SALKA

First published in 2025
by Faber & Faber Limited
The Bindery,
51 Hatton Garden,
London, ECIN 8HN
faber.co.uk
and
Profile Books Ltd
29 Cloth Fair, London EC1A 7JQ

Typeset in Adobe Caslon Pro by Faber
Printed by CPI Group (UK) Ltd, Croydon CR0 4YY

All rights reserved
Text © Francesca Simon, 2025

The right of Francesca Simon to be identified as author of this
work has been asserted in accordance with Section 77
of the Copyright, Designs and Patents Act 1988

A CIP record for this book
is available from the British Library

ISBN 978–0–571–39612–2

Printed and bound in the UK on FSC® certified paper in line with our continuing
commitment to ethical business practices, sustainability and the environment.
For further information see faber.co.uk/environmental-policy

Our authorised representative in the EU for product safety is
Easy Access System Europe, Mustamäe tee 50, 10621 Tallinn, Estonia
gpsr.requests@easproject.com

2 4 6 8 10 9 7 5 3 1

SALKA

FRANCESCA SIMON

ff P

For Gavin Higgins, who told me the story of *The Faerie Bride* and wrote the music, and Marta Fontanals-Simmons and Roderick Williams, who sang it so magnificently.

SALKA

I knew how it would end.
I warned him and warned him.
Faeries and humans — our worlds are separate.
Divided by the lake.
Dangerous to mix.
But would he listen? When has a reckless, love-struck boy ever listened to his mother?

ANGHARAD

I only heard what I wanted to hear.
I forgot every warning.
The moment I saw her face.
The moment I breathed her water lily scent.
The moment I heard her siren song...
I was lost.

              OWAIN

SPRING

SALKA

My father says, 'Don't let them see you. Never let them see you.'

But where's the fun in that?

'Salka!' My father takes my face in his hands. I am not listening, and he knows it. So he tries again. 'Don't play with humans. Stay hidden.'

Doesn't he get bored repeating himself? I've heard this so many times before.

My father is old – old even in the world of the Tylwyth Teg and that is saying something. He lacks an antic disposition. He might as well be a rock or a barnacle for all the spirit of adventure he has left in him. He's seen me hovering just below the surface of the Lake, and he does not like it.

But I like to spy. I like to peek. I like watching humans stand at the water's edge, peering into its bottomless depths. What are they trying to see? Are they hoping to uncover our jewelled kingdom? Maybe spot a water nymph or a pixie? Good luck with that. We are well hidden. Try as hard as you like, unless *we* choose, you'll never see us.

I have such powers! I can make you doubt your eyes. A swish, a shimmering movement in the water like a shoal of fish. What was that? The blue-grey waters shiver, and I am gone.

I never tire of this game.

Humans call my faerie kingdom the Otherworld, but really, as far as we're concerned, *they* live in the Otherworld. They just don't know it.

The Lake is the portal through which the Tylwyth Teg come and go, the doorway between the mortal world and mine. My home is the twilight land beneath the water, where I have always lived.

Humans are trapped in their world of mud and air. But, like all the fair folk, I can glide up from my faerie land through the Lake and back again as easily as any fish.

Best of all, when the moon is full and mist shape-shifts over the water, my family and I rise from the depths to dance in the lush grass. Any human who wanders near our circle, we grab and pull into our revels.

Sometimes we let them go.

Sometimes not.

OWAIN

I am a quiet person. I've never been one for dancing, or fighting on market days, or falling down drunk at fairs. My friend Gareth teases me for daydreaming, but I don't mind. When I sing, I sing for myself alone.

I try to make our farm, Esgair Llaethdy, pay, but it isn't easy. Luck peeked in our door and hopped off elsewhere. Year after year, my mother's frowns get deeper, her hands more gnarled. She stretches out our food as best she can. She tends our remaining cows with fierce affection. I think she loves them more than she loves me, but they are sickly children. Every year our sheep are fewer and fewer, and our thin cows, who have to make do with gorse and ferns when our hay crop is sparse, give less and less milk. Wolves, disease, maggot foot, death in snowdrifts and cliff-falls have decimated our flocks. Without the kindness of our neighbours, who loaned us a ram and brought over a few ewes in a poor exchange for a sack of potatoes and my mother's woollen blankets, we would have no sheep.

We are not the only ones in Myddfai who live poor. I always hope that things will change for the better. I am young and strong, and hard work has never frightened me.

My life has always been as fixed and as steady as the seasons. The rhythm of my days follows the sun and the sheep. Spring for the lambs; summer for shearing and hay-making and hoping the rains hold off until the hay is safe inside; autumn for ploughing, mating the ewes and repairing the dry stone walls which fall down in every gale; winter for hauling hay to the flocks in the high pastures and praying not too many die.

I love these hills, these green and brown valleys, these woods of oak and ash. I love the hushed forests in autumn, the leaves changing colour, the earth turning in on itself. I love spring and summer, when nature is feasting. I love the smell of the black earth, the sheep after shearing, the gathered hay rolled into bales. I love my village of Myddfai.

But most of all, I love the lake. My magical place, with its glittering blue-grey water and red pebbly shore. The way the water reflects the sky, ice blue or flint grey, sunbeams dancing on the surface, moonlight glinting on the secret depths. At sunset, my favourite time, when the lake mirrors a glowing sky, the reeds waver in the breeze, and wild geese drift on the wondrous water.

Here, by Llyn y Fan Fach, I can sit or sing while my sheep graze on the sweet grass of the surrounding hills, and dream of other places, other worlds.

SALKA

I've seen him before. Of course I have. I love watching him singing, trailing his fingers in the water, calling to his wandering sheep.

Humans tread heavily on the land. This boy of earth moves with the lightest step as he walks along the shore.

He doesn't know I am watching him spinning and cartwheeling while his sheep graze on the hills ringing my Lake. Then he pulls off his shirt and lies in the sun, his lean, hard body sleek as an otter except for the flutter of dark hair around his belly.

I can't take my eyes off him. His black curls, his wide dark eyes, brown like silt. I've never seen brown eyes before. His narrow waist, his dirt-smudged cheeks, his lightly freckled nose. Even his ears, coming almost to a point, enchant me.

How is it possible someone so glorious walks on the earth?

He is the most beautiful being I have ever seen.

OWAIN

I have never thought to ask for more.

I am a shepherd. I am a farmer. I will live and die in these black hills.

SALKA

How can I resist that bright face, those strong arms, that crooked smile? The way his fingers trace the water, like he is painting a picture. The way he scratches his dog's head and laughs when the black and white collie crouching beside him shoots off to round up a straying sheep. My fingers yearn to grab his ankles and pull him deep down into the Lake.

I stop myself. That's not how I can have him.

Every day I linger just below the surface to gaze at him.

I watch the giddy valley girls who pretend to bump into him by accident, and wiggle and pose as they hoick their skirts high to show their legs as they dip their toes into my Lake, shrieking at the cold. I can see these hair-tossing, skirt-lifting minxes hold no interest for him, and I am glad, so glad. Hussies. Vixens. Do they think their thick ankles and scratched legs will lure him? He kneels down and strokes his collie while they prance before him. *Go on,* I urge them, *venture further into the waters, so I can pinch your feet – or worse.* Milksops. Dishclouts. He's a god on earth. My glorious boy sits all day on the shore by the water's edge, where our worlds meet. He hugs his knees, leaning his cheek upon his hand. His fingers are long and slender. And always, always, he gazes into my Lake, trying to see my shadow land beneath the water.

I keep myself hidden. I'll decide when to show myself. *If* I show myself.

But I know it's only a matter of time. I am dizzy with love. The fiery fever inside me churns my blood, aches my heart. I can't eat. I can't sleep. To touch him, to walk with him, to lie with him – I have no other thoughts.

I think I will die if he is not mine.

OWAIN

Every day in fine weather I bring the sheep to graze on the mossy green hills surrounding Llyn y Fan Fach. The flock scatter across the slanting cliffs, and Mati keeps an eye on them and stops them wandering off.

There is a flat stone that catches the sun, where I like to eat my lunch of bread and cheese, and then stretch out to rest, or dance, or turn cartwheels where no one can see. The sheep don't care, and Mati is more interested in the sticks I throw for him. I watch the herons and cormorants skidding on the lake's surface, the breeze ruffling their feathers, enchanted by the light playing over the jewelled water.

And then one spring day, when it is summer in the sun and winter in the shade, and the lake is glowing smooth as glass beneath a bright blue sky, I am sitting on the shore eating barley bread when Mati growls.

I look up.

And there she is, sitting on the water, singing and combing her long hair. She peers into the lake, like it's a mirror, combing and combing her black hair, the ends trailing in the shining water and swirling around her.

Then she looks up.

SALKA

His face! I try not to laugh. I ignore him for as long as I can. Then I peek.

He stares at me. I stare at him. Oh, I am bold. I am breaking every law, every taboo.

Open-mouthed, trembling, he holds out his hand.

OWAIN

I hold out my hand to offer her my half-eaten bread, like she is a swan who might feed from my hand.

I don't know why I did that.

The bread was in my hand and I offered it.
I have nothing else. I don't know what to do. I can't speak. My throat is dry. A girl, sitting on the water. But not just a girl. The most beautiful girl I have ever seen.

I keep thinking, *I am not seeing this. How can someone sit on water?* I blink, and she is still there, still sitting on the water, still combing her hair, the sunlight glinting in a million points of light. And then, somehow, she stands and glides over to me, dainty-toed, walking on water in her bare feet, her silky grey dress flowing to her ankles. She comes closer, and closer, her face serious and still. I breathe her water lily scent. I feel faint. I don't want her to leave. I don't want to leave. I'm afraid she will vanish. I want to cry out, *Stay, stay, for God's sake stay.* But I say nothing. I can say nothing.

All I can do is hold out some bread.

She fixes me with her lake eyes, blue green grey.

Then she speaks.

Her voice is silver and moss.

'*Cras dy fara.*

Nid hawdd fy nala.'

Your bread is hard.

It's not easy to catch me.

Then she vanishes beneath the water, leaving me staring, stupid as a cow, at the ripples she leaves in her wake.

What have I done? Why has she fled?

'Come back!' I cry out. 'Come back.'

I've insulted her. I offered her some hard old bread. What an idiot. What a fool. What was I thinking? She deserves gold and silver and jewels, and I offered . . . bread.

SALKA

The bread! The bread! As if I care if his bread is hard or soft, barley bread or sour dough. I didn't come close to him because I want his bread. Does he think I'm a hungry carp? I let him see me because I want him with every fibre of my being.

I am wild.

It's not easy to catch me.

But I will die if I can't have him.

I am Tylwyth Teg. I am not one of his valley girls, drooling and panting over him like a sick sheep.

I swim in circles, up, down. I feel frantic and my heart is racing. The fever I felt the first time I saw him has not abated and burns within me. My twilight world, my Lake life, feels like a dream rippling through my hands.

All I can think about is him.

All I care about is him.

All I dream about is him.

'Are you sea-changed, Salka?' says my twin sister, pulling my hair. 'You let a man see you. You spoke to a human. You walked on the water. I saw you! If Father finds out, you are gutted fish.'

'You're jealous,' I say.

'Of a landslug's love? As if.'

'He is the most beautiful man I have ever seen. Go on, admit it. You've never seen anyone so handsome.'

My sister avoids the question but I know she can't deny what I have said.

'What are you going to do?'

I hesitate. If I say the words I can't take them back.

She studies my face. It's always been easy for her to read me.

'You can't mean this,' she says.

'I do,' I say, deciding in that moment.

'Why would you want to live with *them?*' she asks. 'Pull him down here.'

'You know I can't do that.'

'Why not?'

'Remember? You grabbed a man by the ankles and pulled him down into the depths.'

'He thrashed like a fish, and then he stopped,' she says. 'I remember. We poked and tickled him but . . .' She shrugs. 'I was only playing.'

I don't care about a human who drowned long ago. I take my sister's hand and place it on my heart.

'I am in love. Fathoms deep in love. I am sick with love-longing. I have to be with him.'

'You're bewitched.'

I shake my head.

'You don't know him,' she says.

'What do I need to know? He enchants me.'

And yet.

And yet.

Will I put myself in danger and take bread from his hand? I know if I eat, I will be part of his world. Should I give up my home, and my family, and the faerie life I have always lived, the only world I know, for a shepherd boy with a crooked smile and eyes as brown as silt?

She looks at me. Her eyes fill with tears.
'Salka. Don't leave us.'
I dart away from my sister. I need to think.
I am wild.
It's not easy to catch me.

OWAIN

I run to my home through the heather-covered Ox Eye Moor, down into the valley of the Sow's Mouth, and up the long hogback across the fields to our farm we have nicknamed Uphill House but is really called Long Ridge Dairy.

I leap over the peat sled. I can jump as high as the house.

'Mother!' I say. I push open the door. 'Mother! I have met the girl I am going to marry.'

Her face brightens. She is knitting in her chair by the fire, a shawl over her shoulders despite the heat. There is stew boiling on the hearth and vegetables scattered on the table.

'You've asked Nefyn at last.' She is beaming. 'I hoped and prayed you would. Don't worry, I will move to the downhill cottage, leave you two—'

'No!'

'We always said that when you married—'

'Not Nefyn.'

Her face falls.

'I always hoped you'd marry Nefyn. Join up the farms.'

'That was Nefyn's wish. And her mother's. And yours. Not mine. Never mine.'

My mother pulls her old shawl tighter around her shoulders. When did her arms get so thin? She leans over and pokes the embers. She looks up, arranges her face.

'You're my son, and I will welcome your wife and wish you happiness. Who is she?'

I tell her. I want to dance and sing. I can't stop smiling.

My mother's face clouds. For a moment I think she is going to faint.

'Owain, no. Leave her. No good can come when you marry away.'

'I can't.'

'I am plaguey feared. Humans and faeries shouldn't mix. They're thieves. They change our children for theirs. You know how anyone suspected of having faerie blood is treated around here. How would we explain her? How could we hide who she is?'

My mother's words sail past me, like chaff floating in the wind.

'We'll find a way. I love her,' I say. 'Oh Mum, I love her.'

'How can you love her? You don't even know her.'

'What do I need to know?' I say. 'I saw her. I know her.'

'Ever since you were little, I've warned you: beware the thick mist on the meadows when the moon shines brightly, lest you stumble across the fair folk dancing and be carried off to their land beneath the lake. And now you want to bring one of them here?'

My mother always sees catastrophe.

'I haven't been carried off, Mother, as you can see,' I tell her. What do I care for my mother's warnings? What does she know?

'And yet she didn't come to you,' says my mother.

'No,' I admit. 'She said my bread was hard and that it was not easy to catch her.'

'Forget her,' says my mother. 'Leave her to the lake. Owain, you are only eighteen. What's the rush?'

'You were married at eighteen.'

'Then marry Nefyn. Stick to your own.'

I shake my head. 'I love her. Oh God, I love her. I have never been so certain of anything in my life.'

I close my eyes. Her face. Her hair. Her voice. Her siren song.

I am lost.

I have to marry her.

ANGHARAD

Oh my son, what madness has overtaken you?
Faeries and humans, our worlds are separate.
Divided by the lake. Dangerous to mix.
    Leave the Otherworld alone.
    Why won't he listen to me?

OWAIN

The next day I try again.

My lady of the lake said my bread was hard. This time I grabbed some raw dough rising in the covered proving trough by the fire. The dough is sticky in my hand. I sniff the yeasty smell, then scrunch it into a ball and put it in my pocket. My mother comes down the creaking oak staircase and silently watches me leave.

'Be careful,' she whispers.

I leave the flock out in the fields above our farmhouse and hurry through the morning mist up the sloping green hills to the lake. I am too restless to settle on the shore. I patrol up and down, shielding my eyes from the sun, watching the shining water, listening to the lake's low hum.

And then suddenly, she is there, sitting on the sparkling surface, the breeze lifting her soft hair.

She is even more beautiful than I remember. I want to dive into the lake and swim to her. But I'm frightened she will flee from me again if I get too close.

I hold out the raw dough.

'Oh come, come,' I whisper to myself.

She glides over to me, silent as a swan. Her silky dress swirls around her.

She stops just out of reach, the water bubbling at her feet.

I can't breathe. I must be mad, thinking she would ever marry me. Who am I? A shepherd boy with a few skinny cows and maggoty sheep, a field of potatoes and an arthritic mother.

I lean over the water, hold out the dough.

'For you,' I say.

She smiles, shaking her head, her long black hair glistening.

'*Llaith dy fara.* Your bread is wet,' she says. 'I am wild. It's not easy to catch me.'

Then she disappears back under the water, here and not here, only ripples marking where she had been.

But she smiled at me. I didn't imagine it. She smiled at me.

I throw the dough into the lake. Fish scurry to grab it.

I will try again tomorrow.

And the next day, and the next.

I will spend my life here, sitting by the lake, calling to her, if that's what it takes to win her.

SALKA

Raw dough! Full marks for trying, my love, but really? Why would I be enticed by a lump of raw dough? Is this the gift that humans offer one another when they are besotted?

But what do I care? Raw, baked, barley bread, sour: I know whatever bread he brings me is a love token. I saw him again, and his beauty is undimmed.

I want him more than ever.

I caress his image in my mind over and over: his crooked smile as he leant over the water, enticing me, enchanting me. And oh, how I wanted to go to him, to take his bread, to take his hand, to feel his body pressed against mine, to leave my Lake and be with him, always.

Ond rydw i'n wyllt.
Nid hawdd fy nala.

But I am wild.
It's not easy to catch me.

OWAIN

'No luck?' says my mother, when I return alone that evening. She is spinning wool by the dim candlelight but she doesn't need light to guide her fingers as they draw out the yarn.

I shake my head.

My mother pauses for a long moment. Then she grabs the rusty, long-handled shovel and pulls a fresh loaf from the fire. 'Try this,' she says. 'It's half-baked. Neither raw nor hard. Maybe this will please her more.'

That's all she says, but I know this means she will welcome my faerie bride.

I hug her. I suddenly feel so hopeful I want to cry.

'Thank you,' I say.

'You're my son, my only,' she says. 'I want you to be happy.'

I sit at the table, and my mother hands me a wooden bowl of salt meat broth and carrots. She's added apple dumplings, to make the broth go further. I eat, but my mind is at the lake, with my faerie bride, who I hope and pray will be there tomorrow, waiting for me.

SALKA

I tell Father that if the boy comes again I will be his. That I will give up everything for a human boy with a crooked smile and eyes as brown as silt.

My father begs me to reconsider. Tells me I'm a fool. That I'm fevered. That our faerie world will pull at me, softly and then harder and harder. That I will live with regret.

I won't, I say. I love him. I am exultant. I want to sing and laugh and cry all at once. My life is beginning.

Of course Father has conditions. I know better than to protest. Some things can be changed, and others can't.

It's important to know the difference.

OWAIN

On the third day, I stand on the shore and hold out the half-baked bread. The lake glows turquoise in the light, mirroring the cloudless sky.

Everything is still. I hold my breath, and the world holds its breath with me. No birdsong. No church bells. No herons skimming the water.

Just her, and me, and the lake.

Suddenly, she is there, walking on the water. She comes to me so softly her feet make no din.

I hold out the half-baked bread. She comes closer and closer, so close I can breathe her water lily scent.

Then she reaches out, takes the bread from my hand, and she eats.

SALKA

I eat his soft bread, and smile and smile and smile.

OWAIN

She smiles at me with her lake eyes, blue green grey. And I tell her, 'I will die unless you stay. I love you more than my life. I love you more than my farm. More than these black hills, more than these valleys. I will love you forever.'

And then she says words I have heard in my dreams, and others I don't understand.

SALKA

I will live upon the earth with you.
   I will marry you.
   I will love you.

OWAIN

I feel light-headed. My eyes fill with tears. Can this really be happening? A girl like her, in love with a boy like me?

I reach out to her, longing to touch her.

'Hear me,' she says, stepping back. 'There is one condition.'

'Anything,' I say.

SALKA

'If you strike me three blows—'

He stops me. His face is pale with horror.

'Strike you? *Strike* you? Not one blow. Not ever. I love you. I will never hurt you. How could you think—'

'Listen to me,' I say. 'If you strike me three blows, I must return to the Lake forever.'

He waves his hands, shaking his head.

'Not one blow. Not ever.'

Does he hear me? Does he understand me?

'If you strike me three blows, I must return to the Lake forever.'

OWAIN

I hear, and I don't hear, the words beneath her words. I watch as she rises from the lake, her gleaming black hair flowing down her back, the water brushing her bare feet.

My faerie bride.

My wondrous wife.

And behind her a grey-bearded man, wearing a wreath of lilies, rises out of the water and walks towards me.

'You mean to marry my daughter,' he says. His voice is rock-rough, the sound of pebbles rolling on the shore.

'Yes,' I say. I am too tongue-tied to say more.

Her father sighs, the murmur of wind rustling the reeds.

'Treat her well. Be a kind and faithful husband. She is giving up our world for yours.'

'I will love her till the day I die,' I say.

'Here is her dowry,' says her father. 'As many cows, horses, pigs, sheep as she can count in one breath will be hers.'

She laughs and begins her count.

'One, two three, four, five; one, two, three, four, five; one, two, three, four, five . . .'

And as she counts, a great multitude of cows, horses, pigs, sheep rise from the lake. Like no beasts I've ever seen. So fine, so fair, so fat, so lustrous. I am speechless with awe.

The dowry of my wondrous wife. My faerie bride.

'Will you come to our wedding?' I ask. I imagine for a moment what people will say, when this faerie from the Otherworld appears in our village church.

'You are already married according to our custom,' he replies. 'A dowry given and accepted. Daughter, farewell.'

He sinks back into the lake and vanishes as if he had never been.

Everything is happening so fast.

She steps onto the shore and shakes out her damp hair. I reach out my trembling hand and she takes it.

Her soft hand is cool in mine.

Suddenly she laughs. Her laugh is bells and rippling water.

'I don't know your name,' she says. 'What's your name?'

'Owain,' I say. I feel so shy I can only glance at her. Her beauty blinds me. Is this a dream? I pray I will never wake.

'Owain,' she repeats. My name in her mouth.

'Owain. My Owain.'

I breathe. I think my heart will stop, it is beating so fast.

'I am Salka.'

A shimmery name as shiny and beautiful as she.

'Salka.' Her name tastes sweet on my tongue. 'What does that mean?'

'My name is the sound of water rushing through reeds at daybreak when the mist clears and the first fingers of light reach into the Lake,' she says.

'Oh,' I say.

She takes my hand, puts my finger to her lips and wets it with her tongue. I begin to tremble.

We tumble together to the mossy ground.

Afterwards, we lie there, naked, breathing hard, our limbs entwined. I inhale her water lily scent, cover her face, her neck, her breasts with kisses. I cannot stop trembling.

'I will love you forever and ever.'

'I will love you forever and ever.'

'Do you know me now?' she says, twinning my fingers in hers.

'I know you.'

Salka sits up. Around us there is only the hum of bumblebees, the faint chime of church bells, a trill of birdsong. The warm air bathes us.

'What's that singing?' she asks.

I sit up, pulling on my shirt. I have never heard birds singing by the lake before.

'That's a mistle thrush.'

'Ah. I've only ever heard the honking geese and kingfishers on my Lake.' Salka beams. 'They are singing for us. And in return one day I will come back here and sing to them.'

SALKA

My boy. My beautiful, glowing, magical boy. We steal little glances at each other, as if we can't believe that the other is really there. He smells sweetly, of sheep and earth and wind and sun.

Sun! I have never felt its warm rays on my naked body before. I want to stretch out and bask in the unfamiliar heat, but I know that Owain is keen to take me home.

How strange it is, to look down at the Lake from the land. A curtain of blue water pulled across my twilight world, hiding everything and everyone. As I dress, I wonder for a moment if my sister and father are looking up at me, as I am looking down on them. The brilliant blue sky, the brilliant blue Lake.

The skylake. The lakesky.

I won't look again.

The sun dips lower and the lake glows in the afternoon light like a golden plate.

It's as if the world up here rejoices in my happiness.

OWAIN

I whistle to Mati, who bounds up, thrilled with his new charges. He races around, gathering up the strays. My skinny sheep look bony next to Salka's plump and gleaming beasts.

Salka is sure-footed on the mossy banks, as we head to the farm.

'Will you be all right walking? You don't have shoes.'

'I never wear shoes.'

'I hope you won't miss—'

She puts her soft hand on my mouth. 'My life now is here, with you. It's you. Only you.'

'Will you grow old here?'

'I will grow old here, with you, because I love you,' she says.

I pull her tightly to me. My Salka. My faerie bride. Of all the men in the world, she has chosen me.

Hand in hand, fingers intertwined, we walk together in the sunlight across fields and tree-fringed meadows edged with yellow gorse, through beechwoods purple with bluebells, and groves of oak and ash, up to my farm.

Her marvellous dowry of horses, cows, pigs, sheep follow us. A joyful procession from her world to mine, from one world to another.

SALKA

'Mother, we're home,' Owain calls, pushing open the warped wooden door, then standing back and ushering me in. 'This is Salka.'

I look around his cottage with its worn chairs, the sputtering hearth fire, the settle with its ancient cushions. I touch the uneven stone walls. I pick up the earthenware jug on the table by the little window. I breathe in the warm, musty, drowsy air, see the dust shimmering in the shafts of sunlight which dapple the flagstone floor.

There is soup bubbling in an iron cauldron above the fire. Oatcakes dry on their rack in front of the hearth.

And I think, I am home. At last, I am home. I want to weep, I am so happy.

OWAIN

I see my home through her eyes, how poor it is, how worn out, how unfit for her. The dusty harvest knot from last year hanging from the kitchen rafter. The low, black oak-beamed ceiling pocked with woodworm. The spider webs. The cracked and bare stone floor. The rusty pots. The splintered shepherd's crook.

She must have expected better. She must have lived in realms of gold.

I never even told her I lived with my mother, who puts down her knitting and comes towards us.

SALKA

I wouldn't care if he lived with twenty mothers
and every single one of our cows, pigs and sheep.
   So long as he was here with me.

ANGHARAD

I saw at once she'd bewitched him. His eyes follow her as she looks around the cottage, touching a jug, brushing her fingers along the settle. You'd think she'd never seen a fire or a broom before, the way her eyes widen as she slowly takes in the room.

I don't think he quite believes that she is here. That she has chosen him. Owain has never known how golden and glorious he is.

I am not surprised. Who could resist him?

I move forward to embrace her and she steps back. I drop my arms. I see at once she is not used to being touched.

This is new for us all.

Salka has a tang of the lake. I look into her cool eyes and I see her otherness. She is so beautiful it is unworldly.

She is Tylwyth Teg.

She is not like us.

'I'm sorry, I've no special meal prepared for you,' I say. 'Just some bacon and tatties. And cheese,' I babble. 'We've got barley bread and milk and cheese. We're out of eggs, I'm sorry. I wasn't expecting you.'

Salka smiles, and says nothing.

'Sit, sit,' I urge.

I notice Salka is careful not to take my seat by the hearth. I like that. Nor does she lift the sleepy cat out of his chair, but chooses one further away, against the wall by the linen chest. She is barefoot. Could her family not afford shoes? I always thought faeries were rich.

'You've not brought any clothes with you?'

She shakes her head.

'Not to worry, we will sort you out,' I say, trying to think which of my old dresses is least tattered.

There's nothing. I will have to make her a new dress.

'Will there be a wedding?' I ask.

'We are already wed according to her custom,' Owain says.

'But what will we tell the neighbours?' I say. 'You know how people talk.'

Owain shrugs. 'Say we wed quietly in her land. It's the truth.'

I think of all the gifts I've given to newlyweds over the years – the salt cellars and pepper boxes, the mustard pots, the saucepans, the hens, the flour sacks – the money I could ill afford, telling myself that one day it would all be repaid to my son on his wedding day.

And now he's thrown that all away, with his faerie bride and faerie wedding. There will be no money and no gifts to set up a household for them. No fiddles and harps will play him and his bride to church. I will feel shame when I walk to market or through the village.

Owain sees my downcast face. 'Salka's dowry is already grazing in our pastures and fields, Mother. We're no longer a ten-cow farm, thanks to her bounty.' He breaks into a smile. 'Mother, Salka has given us so much. You've never seen such horses and cows, such sheep and pigs.'

I frown. Dowry or no dowry, if only he'd married Nefyn, joined our farms together, everything comfortable and as it should be.

I keep my thoughts to myself.

The world is turned upside down.

'Tell no one she is of faerie blood,' I say.

'Mother!' says Owain.

Salka is quiet and serene. She walks over to Owain and threads her hand in his.

He raises her pale white hand to his lips. A hand I can tell has never toiled. He gazes at her, glowing with love. Their happiness fills the room. Late afternoon sunlight pouring through the open doorway haloes them.

I can tell they are longing to be alone.

I am in the way.

I pick up my shawl, swap my slippers for clogs.

'Let me go see these wonderful beasts Salka has brought us while there's still light,' I say.

I am not even out the door before they have escaped to Owain's bedroom.

SALKA

Owain is standing naked by the window in the dawn light, his back to me, splashing water from a bowl and jug over his face. The bed is warm from his body. I stretch out and watch him wash his face, his arms, between his legs.

I think I could lie here and look at his body forever.

OWAIN

'Are there people here?' calls our neighbour
Blodwen the next morning, walking through the
open doorway. 'I've brought you some eggs . . .'
She stops, stares at Salka.

And so it begins.

Salka is cool like water. I feel strong with her
beside me.

'Blodwen, this is my wife, Salka,' I say, my voice
stumbling in wonder over the word 'wife' – the
first time I have ever said it.

Blodwen's ruddy face goes pale. Like my
mother, she'd always hoped I would marry
her daughter, Nefyn. I see her quick glance at
Salka's belly. She is so shocked, she forgets to
congratulate me.

'Well now,' she says. 'You're a secret one,
Owain.'

I smile. I am so happy. I want to sing and dance and run through the fields shouting for joy and kicking my heels like a colt. I am so in love I can barely hold myself together.

I feel kindly towards the world, even towards an old gossip like Blabby Blodwen.

'Where are you from, Salka?'

'I'm from the—' she starts to answer.

'Salka comes from away,' I interrupt. 'From across the water.'

'Not a valley girl. I didn't think so,' says Blodwen. 'I've never been further than the mountain. My late husband went as far as Caenarvon once. But not me. What's over there that's not here?'

Blodwen is unsure what to do. Normally she'd make herself comfortable on the settle by the hearth, or sit on the bench at the table. Instead, she stands, holding her battered metal egg basket in front of her like a shield.

'You've come a distance, so.'

'For Owain I would travel the world,' says Salka.

For once Blabby Blodwen does not live up to her name.

'I'll be off then,' she says. 'The cows won't milk themselves.'

She heads for the door, still clutching her basket, her clogs clip-clopping on the stone floor.

'The eggs?' says my mother.

Blodwen shakes her head and empties her egg basket into ours.

We all know it's too early to milk the cows. She wants to spread the news in the village. Godspeed to her feet – the more she blabs, the less we will have to explain.

SALKA

The moment the red-faced neighbour with the bad lungs and swollen heart leaves, I speak.

'Why can't you say who I am? I am Salka from the Lake, like you are Owain from Esgair Llaethdy. I don't come from across the water. I come *from* the water.'

'I know. And I love you for it with every breath in my body,' says Owain. He comes over and wraps me in his arms. I lean against his chest. 'But not everyone thinks humans and faeries should mix. I want to protect you.'

'From what?'

'From . . . them. People here don't like outsiders.'

'Why not?'

Owain and his mother look at one another.

'The people here in Myddfai . . .' Owain begins.

'They are frightened of faerie folk,' says his mother.

'I don't understand. I mean them no harm.'

'Of course you don't. Of course you don't,' says Owain.

'Your ways are other,' says Angharad. 'People say the fair folk steal children and change them for faerie ones who grow up peevish and deformed.'

I am astounded. 'Why would we want a human child? Our own are much fairer.'

'There is no reasoning with them,' says Owain.

'If they know who you are, they'll never accept you,' says his mother.

She knows who I am, and I know that she is struggling.

'I am Tylwyth Teg,' I say. 'That is who I am.'

'I wouldn't have you any other,' says Owain. He beams at me. 'My faerie bride. My wondrous wife. Don't worry,' he adds. 'When people get to know you, they will love you as I do.'

BLODWEN

How could Owain do this to Nefyn, to me, to Angharad? Marry some stranger and bring her here?

He's ruined everything.

NEFYN

Owain should have been mine.
    That's all I will say.

SALKA

'Will there be dancing?' I ask. Angharad wants to have a party, to celebrate our marriage.

Owain hugs me. 'There will be dancing, my darling! And singing! And rejoicing!'

I smile at him. 'I love to dance,' I say.

I am going to be so happy here.

OWAIN

Bells are ringing. An archway of wild flowers lines the entrance to the tavern, decked with streamers and pennants. Salka and I walk together under the arch, flowers strewn on our path. Salka's dress shines like stars.

The tables are pushed back, fresh rushes cover the floor, candles twinkle. There is wine, beer, hot spiced ale, cakes, biscuits. Food has never tasted so fine, so sweet.

Salka spins a golden light around her, around us, a circle of joy and wonder. Oh my beloved, I think I will burst with love for you.

The entire village has come. There isn't enough room for everyone inside, so the dancing spills out into the meadow. I see everyone watching us, all my friends marvelling at her, my Salka, so beautiful, so radiant, so dainty-toed. How did I ever come to be so blessed?

We're dancing and laughing and smiling at one another and I think I will never again be as happy as I am tonight, dancing with my faerie bride.

SALKA

We dance and we dance, circling and clapping. The villagers come over, shy, claim a dance. I dance with them all, man and boy. I would dance with the oxen and the sheep, I am so filled with joy. When at last Owain takes my hand and we whirl together to the merry sound of the fiddle and the harp, I feel giddy with love for everyone and everything, but most of all for Owain, my beautiful Owain, my wondrous boy.

ANGHARAD

I watch the dancing, the drinking, the cautious eyes following Salka. I wanted to have a wedding feast and celebrate their marriage, not hide Salka from the village as if we are ashamed. Salka's dowry makes all this possible. I've brought everyone over to greet my new daughter-in-law, presented her proudly. I will not stand for any frost. What *I* think of what Owain has done, I keep to myself.

Old Erin limps over to me, her daughter Lowri hovering close beside.

'Strange we've never seen her before,' says Old Erin.

'Salka comes from away,' I say, tapping my feet to the jigs Anwyn and Siriol play. 'Lowri, you should be dancing.'

Lowri rolls her eyes. 'I've got two left feet. I'm

always crashing into everyone,' she says.

'Ask Salka to teach you,' I say. 'I never saw a girl so lively and lithe.'

Lowri looks as if I've scalded her.

'I know you'll make her welcome,' I say loudly, speaking over the music.

Erin and Lowri say nothing.

'Shame not to marry a Myddfai girl,' says Old Erin.

I shrug. 'Owain has always gone his own way.'

'She's pretty, I'll give her that,' says Erin.

'Pretty?' interrupts Terfel. He's swaying, too much to drink. 'She's the best-looking girl who has ever walked this sweet earth.'

'I don't know about that,' I say. 'Myddfai is famous for its beautiful girls.'

Terfel snorts and staggers off.

'Excuse me, I'll be joining the dancing,' I say, and step into the circle.

I still have a jig or two in me.

ANGHARAD

The day after the party, Blodwen comes to visit. Most mornings, after I've seen to my lovely cows, we sit together, knitting stockings. Owain and Salka have gone to turn the sheep out onto the moorland.

'So tell me. Who is she?' says Blodwen. 'What's her family?'

'I don't know,' I say. It's only a half-lie. I've never met her people. 'Why not ask her?' I say.

Blodwen pales. There's something about Salka that invites no questions.

'She's from the fair folk, isn't she?' says Blodwen, lowering her voice.

'I haven't asked,' I say. That's true, of course. I never asked.

'She must be Tylwyth Teg. Just look at her,' says Blodwen, clicking her needles together. 'She's certainly enchanted Owain. I've never seen a man so in love.'

I pinch my mouth tightly. I need to shut down this loose talk.

'Salka is my son's wife. I won't have her shamed.'

'My lips are sealed,' says Blabby Blodwen. 'Her secret is safe with me.'

No one wants to have faerie blood. Blodwen forgets herself.

'There is no secret,' I say. 'Salka comes from away. That is all.'

NEFYN

If they'd married in church like decent people, I would have waited in the front porch when he emerged with that bitch.

I would have cursed him. 'May you rue this day as long as you live.'

I would have had no shame.

But they didn't and my curse is wasted.

No herb of grace for him.

OWAIN

It is early morning, and Salka and I are lying together on the warm, crumpled grass in the high meadows. Mati looks after the sheep, so we have moments of peace and privacy up here, surrounded by hills and sky, with only larks ascending into the sun for company.

I feel like I have been asleep my whole life. Now that Salka is here, every part of my body feels alive. I close my eyes. I can still taste her on my tongue.

Salka teases me. 'All the girls wanted you, you know,' she says, running her fingers across my face and picking out flower petals and bits of sheep's wool which have got tangled in my hair.

I blush. I have always blushed easily.

'Surely not.'

'Oh yes,' she says. 'I've seen how they look at you.'

'It must be because I have all my teeth, and most of the men here only have four.'

'That must be why,' she says, stroking my bare thigh.

I roll over and pull her on top of me.

She laughs, and kisses me hard.

SALKA

Everything is so bright. How do humans not go blind? I am glad that days here are so often rainy and misty. Whenever the sun appears I'm dazzled by the light.

In the Otherworld – which I must now call my home beneath the Lake, though those words are strange to say – I lived in twilight.

So cloudy days and night times are when I feel most at ease. And rain. How I love the rain. I've never felt rain on my body before.

In my first days up here I marvelled at the sun and delighted in its unfamiliar warmth. Now, sometimes, I long for fog and mist and shadows, when the soft dying day melts into night.

OWAIN

What good fortune Salka has brought. Never such oxen, never such cows, never such calves, never such sheep, never such milk and butter and cheese.

Before Salka came, we had a tiny run-down farm. Now our land teems with life. Our butter is creamier than any other in Myddfai, our milk more abundant. Our sheep have finer fleeces and sweeter meat. Our crops burst from the ground.

Even more wondrous, maggots no longer infect our flocks. All our neighbours have lost sheep to maggot infections, but not us. Not since Salka came with her fine flock. Our sheep never go lame now. Our cows never get foul foot.

Flies buzz madly round our neighbours' sheep, but not ours. Somehow, ours are protected.

It's as if my radiant Salka has blessed the farm, as she has enchanted me.

TERFEL

Owain's a lucky bastard. Where'd he find a girl like that? He says she's come from away. Across the water, some say. Maybe there's more like her. Maybe they're *all* like her across the water.

Makes you think.

Maybe I shouldn't have settled for the first girl who winked at me. Loving Elen is like licking honey from a thorn.

NEFYN

I take my washing down to the stream, where
I meet Lowri and Gwen. They too looked at
Owain like I did, tried to catch his eye and more.

Even though he was always meant to be mine.

I vow I will not mention Salka's name, which
cuts my throat like a bramble.

'Have you spoken to her yet?' asks Lowri.

'No.'

They are both clearly longing to say more.

I won't give them the pleasure.

'She's so pretty,' says Lowri.

'Compared to her, we're all crows trooping with
a dove,' says Gwen.

We look glumly at each other. Gwen and
Lowri were my rivals. Now we are united in loss.

What is it they say? Misery loves company.

SALKA

Owain and I are walking the sheep up to fresh pastures. Mati keeps them together, but they can smell the sweet grass that awaits them, and they hurry along the rocky trails.

The green and golden fields are filled with wild flowers and the hum of bees. Skylarks whirl, dipping and swirling in magical shapes, their wings drumming the air. The sweet dusty smell of the hayfields below wafts over us.

My body feels heavy on this land. I can't move with the lightness and speed I am used to.

Everything here is so new, so different. My faerie world, my hidden world beneath the Lake never changed.

I've never known seasons, felt the air start to crisp and chill, the leaves change colour, the nights lengthen as summer slips into autumn.

The birdcalls! I never tire of hearing their voices and learning their songs.

The smells! Of course I knew the smell of animals before. But not like here. Everything on earth is so pungent and the food tastes so odd.

But I love the lush grass, the scent of honeysuckle tangled up in the hedgerows. I still marvel each time I watch the sun rise over the hills and feel the earth warm and alive beneath my feet.

I love seeing the mists veil the high ridges, and the patchwork of fields and farmhouses and hedges.

I love seeing sunbeams dancing on my ice-bright Lake.

But most of all, I love Owain, the boy whose beauty never fails to fell me. Whenever he is near, I stop my work, just to look at him.

My eyes follow him, and his follow me, a dance for the two of us. His beauty binds me tightly to him, like kelp twisted round a rock.

I never knew it was possible to love someone so entirely.

But the villagers in Myddfai.

The villagers.

The villagers never smile. They look me in the eye and some even try to greet me by hugging me. I don't like to touch anyone except Owain, or to feel anyone else's body near mine but his.

Most human bodies (except for my Owain) smell awful. I don't know how to tell them to bathe more. I told Gethin he did not smell good and, rather than thanking me, he got up and left the tavern.

Rhona once asked me if I thought her baby was the prettiest I had ever seen. I said no, her child was ugly.

Why do they expect me to lie?

In my faerie world— No. I won't say it. That is the past and behind me. I will not compare.

I won't even think it.

ANGHARAD

It is said that the Tylwyth Teg bring wealth. It is said truly. I am dazzled by Salka's dowry. Our new flocks cover the hills. We have the most beautiful cows I have ever seen. Their sweet milk pours into my buckets. We have the creamiest cheese and our rich butter is unlike anything I have ever tasted before.

We have gone from poverty to wealth in an instant.

I remind myself of this every day – whenever I hear whispers, or notice her strange ways – to be grateful.

I've taught Salka to bake bread. She learns fast. She sniffs the dough, picks it up and rubs the ball between her hands as if she is stroking a newborn lamb.

It's warm, she says. It's alive. I love that.

SALKA

Nesta has come to our farm to return a peat shovel she borrowed. She stares at my bare feet. Is she checking to see if my toes are webbed?

'You're always barefoot,' she says, wheezing. Her nose is constantly dripping.

'I don't like shoes,' I say. 'They pinch. Why do you wear them?'

Nesta looks down at her clogs. Her trotters are thick, like lumps of marsh mud.

'No one's ever asked me that,' she says. 'I'd have no feet left without my clogs, the amount of tramping I do. Besides, I'm married to the clog-maker. How'd that look, if his own wife shunned his wares?'

I say nothing, wait for her to go.

'Goodbye for now,' she says, waving.

I go back to stretching and kneading the bread

dough. I love the feel of the living dough in my fingers and the yeasty smell. I pull and tug and smooth the warm dough into a floury ball. I place it in the proving trough.

I am getting good at baking barley bread.

NEFYN

She sings strange songs.
    She talks to the cows.
    She dances in the moonlight by the lake.
    How do I know? I've followed her there, I've seen her, I know.
    She is not like us.

SALKA

Sometimes, when Angharad thinks I am not looking, I catch her staring at me. Does she think I am going to vanish in a puff of smoke, or change the pail into a palace?

'Don't worry,' I say. 'I am not so different from you.'

That's a lie, of course.

But there is truth in it.

Angharad's eyes widen, because I have read her thoughts.

ANGHARAD

'Why do people stare when I walk by and then start to whisper?' asks Salka. 'Am I not the bride of the loveliest boy in Myddfai? Don't I bake as well as they – better, in fact, now that my dough isn't so sticky? Don't my animals thrive, and isn't my butter the sweetest?'

'Your ways are other,' I say. 'You must learn to be more like us.'

Salka looks at me as if I have grown three heads.

'No,' says Salka. 'No. Even if I try, I cannot be more like you. I am a faerie.'

What can I do, except watch and hope and pray that somehow all will turn out well? It's bad enough she stands out so much, with her eerie beauty and foreign ways. Her odd manner. Her strange songs. Her habit of wandering alone at night and not saying where she has been.

She still won't wear shoes. She says they pinch.

The clogger is skilled, I say. The alder trees here are soft, and the clogs are comfortable, I promise. 'You'll have no trouble with your feet wearing clogger Rhodri's soles.'

Salka shakes her head, smiling.

'My feet are fine as they are.'

'And when winter comes?' I ask. 'Surely you'll not go barefoot in the snow?'

'What is snow?' she asks.

No good can come when you marry away.

SALKA

No one knows me here. They only know that I am foreign, that I have come from away, even if they don't know I am Tylwyth Teg.

And they don't like it. I scare them.

I will never understand why. They don't scare me. And their ways are as strange to me as mine to them.

NEFYN

'Owain never carved you a love spoon, did he?' says my brother.

'No.'

'Well then,' Gareth says.

I am silent. Must we keep talking about my sorrow?

'There's lots of boys in the village,' my mother says. 'You're not ugly. Take your pick.'

But none like him. Oh God, none like him.

SALKA

When Owain walks into a room, or strolls through a market, or gallops off on horseback, all eyes lock on him. How can he not see this? He is so beautiful, my boy of earth and stars.

Nefyn isn't the only heartbroken one. I see girls and women – and a few men – wed and unwed, sit up when he is around, play with their hair, toss their heads, laugh too loud, ask for his help. He is taller than most of the men here, slim and quick, yet I know he can take on all comers at wrestling, though he does not brag.

I am watching him ripen from boy to young man, his beard start to grow, his muscles to ripple under his shirt sleeves, his almost-finished body my endless pleasure and delight.

At night, when I am restless and cannot sleep, he holds me in his arms and tells me wondrous

stories, of gods and ghosts and kings and queens.
I did not know that his world had stories like
mine.

ANGHARAD

Everything that Salka bakes is better than anything I make. I have watched her prepare our food, and I don't see what she does that is different, but her stews and bacon-stock broths are meatier, her oatcakes fluffier (and never burn), her butter is the sweetest, her milk the creamiest, and whatever mysterious magic she weaves, her food tastes wonderful.

I offered to make her a dress and she said no. Now I understand why. The clothes she weaves are finer, silkier, fall softly around her in ways I can never copy. When she walks, her glistening dresses move with her, almost as if they are interweaved with threads of gold. They are not. I have looked and looked but I cannot uncover the secret.

And her weaving! I've never seen anyone's

fingers fly so quickly over the cloth. She spins yarn and weaves faster than anyone I know.

Now we have fine woollen blankets, soft rugs, warm flannels. Her work is never stiff and rough. All the wool that comes from her sheep is fluffy and silky beyond measure.

Whatever Salka touches becomes a little brighter, a little better, than it was before.

OWAIN

Since Salka came, the most ordinary tasks
– chopping logs, mending walls, fetching water,
moving the sheep between fields, brushing Mati
– are joyful with her beside me, laughing, teasing,
embracing me.

   Sometimes I wake in the middle of the
night and gaze at her, asleep beside me in the
moonlight, her head resting on her arm, her black
hair fanning across the pillow, her naked body
gleaming. I hardly dare to caress her, for fear I
have dreamt her and she will dissolve at my touch.

SALKA

His feet are so warm.

OWAIN

Her feet are so cold. It's like being in bed with ice I've shattered from a frozen ditch in winter.

'You're cold,' I say, grabbing her and rubbing her legs with my feet.

Salka smiles. 'I am never cold.'

Then she kisses me and catches me in her arms. Slowly I unbutton her nightdress. She raises her arms and I lift the gown over her head.

'Dear heart,' she murmurs.

SALKA

I take Owain's hand and place it on my belly. I can feel the flutter of life inside me.

'I'm pregnant,' I say.

Owain starts to cry.

'Why are you crying?' I ask.

'Because I am so happy,' he says. 'Do you need to sit down? Are you well?'

'I am well,' I say. 'We will have a son in the spring.'

'Not a daughter?' says Owain. 'How do you know?'

'I have faerie sight,' I say. 'I know.'

'Then we will call him Rhiwallon, for my father,' he says.

'Better than calling him after my father,' I say. 'You would stand here all day before you had finished saying his name.'

I am sorry I mentioned my father. I don't like to speak about my dead life.

Owain puts his arms around me.

'Do you miss him?' Owain murmurs into my hair.

'No,' I say.

Owain smells of wood smoke and sweet hay. I could stand here with my arms around him and breathe him in forever.

NEFYN

It's happened. I have managed to avoid meeting Salka all summer, dodged her at the hay harvest, and I stayed away from the shepherds' feast. But my luck ran out today when I was working on the peat bog, checking to see if the bricks I'd made last spring were dry enough to collect.

I hear her before I see her. Singing one of her foreign songs. I look up and there she is, walking over the hill. Swinging her damp hair. Smiling her witchy smile.

She sees me and stops singing. Then she continues walking towards me.

For a wild moment I want to swing my shovel at her.

I shove it into the peat.

She looks at me with her strange eyes, as if she can read my thoughts.

Then she says, 'Owain will never be yours. You will never be his. Accept your fate with grace, Nefyn.'

She nods at me and walks on.

Well la-di-da. That's easy for her to say. Stuck-up cow.

The moment she is out of my sight I burst into tears.

GARETH

My sister Nefyn is broken-hearted. But who can blame Owain? Nefyn is a crow compared to Salka. A sulky crow at that.

But still . . . it would have been nice.

I am ploughing, Owain walking beside the heavy grey horses steaming and glistening, their tails trailing in the dirt, their black manes dipping in their eyes as we plod up and down the fields. First Owain's field, and then mine. We've done so together since we were boys.

The horses' chains jangling, plough wheel turning, 'Woah, woah,' I shout, as we plough into the pale sun, mapping and slicing furrows like butter.

'You're happy, Owain?' I say, wiping the sweat from my eyes. It's cold, and winter is coming, but the work is hard and we sweat as if it's blazing with heat.

'So happy,' he says.

'Salka is beautiful,' I say.

Owain smiles. 'I bless the day I saw her.'

I wait for him to say more, but he doesn't.

'Where did you meet her?'

Owain is silent.

'Come on,' I urge. 'You must remember where you first saw her?'

'By the lake,' he says finally.

'On her own?'

Owain looks at me. 'Why all these questions?'

'Is she Tylwyth Teg?' I blurt, before I can stop my words.

Owain stiffens.

'You know how people talk,' I say.

'Never ask me that again,' he says. 'Salka comes from away.'

SALKA

We circle around one another, pulled together by invisible threads. When we are in the same room, we are always close. When we walk the green hills, there is no space between us. His arm around my shoulders, my arm around his waist. His fingers playing with my hair, my hands stroking his face. As if we still can't believe the other is real.

Angharad brings the cows into the new barns at first frost, where she can tend them best, but our hardy sheep, so fat and glossy with their thick coats like no other in the valleys, stay out all winter, warm and damp in the snow. Together Owain and I bring them hay, shatter the ice in the water trough, make sure none have got lost or stuck in a frozen ditch or prickly hedge. He has carved me a fine shepherd's crook, which I treasure.

I love watching Owain with the sheep. His careful hands checking their fleeces and hooves, patting their haunches, scratching their ears. He is so gentle, and so handsome, leaning on his old carved crook as he surveys our fine flocks.

Then he sees me and his face lights up, the way it always does when I am near.

I never knew it was possible to be so happy.

OWAIN

Salka has a way with animals. She whispers to the skittish ewes, and they quiet. The cows follow her willingly. The horses gallop over to nuzzle her. The pigs roll around at her feet. Even Mati, who I raised from a pup, goes to Salka to lay his head on her lap. She murmurs to them, and it's as if they are spellbound.

MATI

Sheep. Sheep. Bad sheep. Good sheep. Keep together. Stay together. Bad sheep. Good sheep.

Wait . . . Watch . . . Head down. Tail up. Go!

Wait. Watch. Head down. Tail up. Go! Keep together. Stay together, baa baas. You go where *I* say.

Who's a good dog?

Me.

My hills. My man. My sheep. My faerie.

OWAIN

Salka won't speak about her life before me. Nor will she say anything about the land beneath the lake.

'That's my dead life,' she says. 'Dead and gone. My living life is here, with you.'

I don't ask her about the faerie world, though I can't help but wonder. Is it really a jewelled kingdom? Are there water nymphs in the lake? Do faeries move amongst us?

I want to forget where she is from.

I'm always frightened that she will leave me, and return to the riches of the Otherworld.

SALKA

Living on the earth and never returning to my
faerie world is the price I pay to be with Owain.
   I pay it gladly, now and forever.
   When I decide something, it is done.
   I never look back.

GARETH

I come right out and ask Owain to borrow a ram.
Our flock is failing and I can't afford to be proud.
   My friend smiles and hugs me.
   Take your pick, he says. And some ewes.
   I am so relieved I could cry. Owain is now so rich I feared he had forgotten what it is like to be poor.

SALKA

I have a friend. I didn't seek her, but she sought me. I try to keep apart from the villagers with their hard eyes and suspicious looks, but this is not always possible.

I was singing to the cows, enjoying their swaying walk down the shady lane back to the farm. I passed Anwyn on the way, who stopped to listen, then she picked up her fiddle and began to play along.

'Will you sing me another song?' she said. So I did.

> *Dacw 'nghariad i lawr yn y berllan,*
> *Tw rym di ro rym di radl didl dal*
> *O na bawn i yno fy hunan,*
> *Tw rym di ro rym di radl didl dal*
> *Dacw'r tŷ, a dacw'r 'sgubor;*

Dacw ddrws y beudy'n agor.
Ffaldi radl didl dal, ffaldi radl didl dal,
Tw rym di ro rym di radl didl dal.

I'd seen Anwyn twice before, playing fiddle at my wedding feast and again in the shearing shed, after all the village flocks were shorn and marked and clipped. But I did not speak to her, and she did not speak to me.

Every so often now, Anwyn comes calling. She is lonely and full of secrets.

At first I was not friendly, but she did not seem to notice. Now I find myself looking forward to her visits.

ANWYN

I've never met anyone like Salka. She's not like the other girls from here. I'm a clumsy cow, and she's lithe as a goat, even with her pregnant belly. No wonder Owain fell in love with her.

I bring my fiddle to her farm, and she sings such songs. Her voice is like bells underwater. She sings sad songs I've never heard, with tongue-twisty words I don't seem to be able to learn, that she says are from her homeland, which must be beyond the mountains.

And she has healing hands. Her knowledge of herbs is wondrous to me. When I was suffering so much with monthly pains and cramps, she gave me angelica root and the pains were eased. She placed her cool hands on my stomach, and I felt the cramps jump from me to her. She gave fennel gum to my father for his weepy eye, and cured him. When Blodwen burned her hand on the fire, Salka smeared crushed river startip mixed with whey on her wound, told her to do so three times daily for nine days, and healed her. When Rhona's baby got pneumonia and looked close to death, Salka gave her sharp dock and the baby recovered.

I write down Salka's marvellous recipes, because her knowledge is so deep and I don't want to forget.

Viper's garlic for wounds and swelling.

Brassica for nettle rash.

Poppy for sleep.

Wormwood mixed with wine to kill pains.

I know I'll never leave these black mountains, and sometimes when we are spinning together Salka tells me stories of magic kingdoms, where kings and queens live in jewelled palaces and water nymphs play. Everyone is rich, and no one is ever hungry or sorrowful.

I could listen to her tales forever.

NEFYN

It breaks my heart to see them together. Laughing, smiling, touching. Owain never looks away from her. He barely notices me any more. I'm just Nefyn, an old broom, a frayed bridle.

That bitch has bewitched him.

Why does she have more gold than I? More beauty? More fame?

I hate her so much. She sings to plants. I've heard her. Strange songs. Foreign songs. Songs from away. Gwen says she swims naked. Sioned says she dances in the dark, when the mist hangs low on the meadows by the lake. Anyone else would be wary of the fair folk, but not her. My mother even saw her dancing in the churchyard and told her to stop. 'But why?' says Salka. 'The dead are glad of the company.'

She is not like us.

I pray every day she will go back to wherever she came from. Maybe she'll die in childbirth.

One can always hope.

I've never loved anyone but Owain. Owain with his little boy smile and faraway eyes.

Owain who was always meant to be mine.

It is torture for me. I think of them at night, curled up together, caressing each other, and I think I will die from grief. I wish I could leave this place, so I wouldn't have to see them, but where would I go? I'm trapped here, living in the farm next to the boy I love, who will never love me.

Why should she be happy, and me so unhappy? He would have married me. I know he would. It's what everyone wanted. And what I wanted.

Why did she have to come?

ANGHARAD

I still wish he had married a Myddfai girl. Nefyn mopes about the fields with a face like a wet week and it hurts me to see her pain.

Get a grip, girl, I want to tell her. Not everyone is lucky in love. Salka is here to stay.

My son will never love you.

OWAIN

Salka insists on walking barefoot, even in winter. I am begging her to wear boots – she attracts too much attention by running in the snow with no shoes. I suggest she wears boots or clogs in winter, and can go barefoot again as soon as spring comes.

Salka refuses.

'For God's sake, Salka, can't you just wear the damn clogs?' I snap at her.

'You aren't listening to me,' she shouts. 'I do not feel the cold. Why are you telling me what to wear?'

This is our first quarrel.

I never thought we would fight about clogs.

Salka finally agrees to let Rhodri come and measure her feet. She will let him make her a pair of clogs.

She will not promise to wear them.

She does not mind if people stare at her, or if people whisper.

But I mind. Even though I shouldn't. I wish she would try harder to fit in.

I will try not to care.

I will try to be more like Salka.

RHODRI

She has the prettiest feet I've ever measured. How does she tramp about barefoot, with delicate feet like that? I took extra care, used my softest alder.

I like knowing that she's wearing my shoes.

SALKA

Owain watches me take a few steps in my new clogs. They hang heavy on my feet. I feel like a hobbled horse, a chained dog.

'Thank you,' says Owain.

We have agreed. I will wear them in winter, but no other season.

Why does it mean so much to him, that I don't stand out?

OWAIN

Salka looks grim in her clogs. You would think I had shod her in iron boots.

I'm trying to protect her. To help her pass. To help her be more like us.

It's not much to ask.

Is it?

ANWYN

'How old are you, Salka?' She is helping me catch our horse, who has bolted from his field.

The question startles her.

'How old are *you*?'

'I'm seventeen,' I tell her.

'So am I,' she says.

OWAIN

Our neighbours gather together in the winter evening cold, peeling rushes and carding wool. Tonight they have come to us. Nefyn, as usual, has not appeared. She's never spoken to me since I brought Salka home.

Salka's stomach is round now, her graceful movements a little slower. She ties her apron higher and higher as her time approaches. The baby kicks and turns in his waterworld. Sometimes I imagine I can hear him.

I sit close beside Salka in the corner carving spoons and ladles, listening to the chatter and throwing peat onto the hearth fire. You learn a lot when you are a quiet man sitting in a chair by the fireside.

'Did you hear about the fight at the fair this morning?' says Elen.

'Ooh, what happened?' says Blodwen.

'You know the lad with the white-blond hair and fair skin?' says Elen. 'Rhys? From the next parish, who sells shovels and sheep shears? Ifan accused Rhys of being Tylwyth Teg. Rhys punched him, and then all hell broke loose. Ifan has a black eye and lost a tooth.'

'There's always been talk about Rhys having faerie blood. Where'd that hair come from, if not from the faeries?' says Lowri.

'I always avoid that Rhys when I see him. No sense in taking the risk,' says Blodwen.

'Ifan should have touched him with iron. That would smoke him out. Everyone knows faeries don't like iron,' says Sioned.

'How can Rhys be Tylwyth Teg?' says my mother. 'He works with iron.'

'Faeries can do all kinds of tricks,' says Nesta. She wipes her runny nose on her sleeve. 'Remember when they bought up all the corn in the market? The price went sky-high.'

'They drag people into their faerie rings and make them dance. Remember when Dylan vanished? The faeries took him,' says Gwen.

'They set fire to the corn in the fields, when my uncle Aled ploughed up their circle,' says Sioned.

'They steal children, you know,' says Lowri. 'They tried that trick with my great-grandmother.'

'The one who threw her changeling baby into the stream? Did the faeries bring hers back?' asks Anwyn.

'No,' says Lowri.

'Then she killed her own baby for nothing,' says Anwyn.

'Rhona has no worries there. Who'd steal her ugly baby?'

Everyone laughs.

Salka does not falter. Her quick fingers card the wool – the fine wool from our fine sheep – better than all others.

'You're quiet as always, Salka,' says Old Erin. 'What do you think?'

Salka looks at Old Erin with her direct, clear gaze.

'I think we will never know,' she says.

SALKA

Of course that's not what I think. But I am learning to hold my tongue. I listen to these women, and I cannot believe their foolish words. Why would we steal their peevish, sickly babes, and swap them for one of ours? Better to blame faeries for their child's harelip or club foot or strange ways than accept it.

And what nonsense about touching iron. I pick up the tongs and poke the embers, aware of eyes on me.

I open my mouth to speak these truths, and then I stop. Something else has caught my attention.

I look closely at Old Erin and I see that death will come for her soon.

'You are old, Erin,' I say.

'Tell me something I don't know, girl,' says

Erin, scowling and drawing her shawl tighter around her thin body.

'You will die after the last lamb is born,' I say.

The room falls silent.

Old Erin stiffens. Her daughter Lowri glares at me. The other women shrink into themselves, pulling away from me as if I were the angel of death. I turn to Angharad. Her face is ashen.

What have I said?

Have I said something wrong?

What is the matter? Why does everyone look so scared?

The women bend over their rushes as if a foul stench has suddenly filled the cottage. The fearful silence feels heavy on my shoulders.

My mother-in-law breaks the silence.

'I saw Rhodri at the market today. He says his cow has started giving milk again.'

I stay silent.

When everyone has gone home, Angharad takes me aside and upbraids me.

'Don't say such terrible things. No one but God knows when we will die.'

'But I know,' I say. 'I have faerie sight. Sometimes I see what is hidden.'

'Keep this to yourself,' says Angharad. 'We will never speak of this again.'

I don't understand. In my world we always want to know the day of our death.

I am not from here.

I am not like them.

ANGHARAD

Why couldn't Owain have married someone else? Anyone else? Salka brings trouble as well as riches in her wake.

OWAIN

Salka has healing hands. Even those who distrust, or even fear her, come to our door for her herbs and tinctures. When one of the cows kicked my mother, Salka applied a potion and the wound healed up fast.

But sometimes . . . her faerie ways are unsettling. I've never been a source of gossip, of rumours, of wary looks before.

She is not like anyone else in Myddfai. It's why I love her, why I am consumed by love.

It's why she allures me.

It's why I don't always understand her.

It's why I am afraid that I will never be enough for her. Who am I after all? A shepherd. I have no special powers, no great wealth or status.

Yet she has given up everything for me. I love her so much I am speechless. With her I am so much more than I ever was.

Salka makes my life worth living. She lights my darkness. I pray she knows that without her, I am driftwood and mud.

Sometimes I don't know where she ends and I begin.

GARETH

If love is a sickness then Owain has it bad. The way he looks at her. The way they lean their bodies together, murmuring and laughing. It's as if he cannot bear to be apart from her.

I feel the heat between them, and I feel cold.

I have never been with any girl but Sioned, but I know I do not feel for her what Owain feels for Salka. Sioned is a nice girl and everyone expects us to marry and so we will. But Owain and Salka are linked together by a fire I will never know.

SIONED

For Gareth's sake, I am making an effort with Salka. They are our closest neighbours, and Owain and Gareth go way back.

There's just something about her I don't like.

Is it because she rarely smiles?

Is it because she never joins in with our laughter and jokes? Does she even know what a joke is? I'm not sure.

Is it her pale skin, which never seems to go brown in the sun like the rest of us?

Or her weird eyes, a colour I have never seen before, a colour that seems to change every time I see her, from blue to green to grey? As if she is not fixed to the earth, that she is shimmery, that she might just vanish and then reappear? I've not seen her do this, but I am watchful for witchy ways.

But I will be friendly. I have promised Gareth.

ANGHARAD

'And how are the lovebirds?' asks Blodwen. Her pitch pot has sprung a leak, and she has come to borrow one of ours, to finish marking her sheep.

'As besotted as ever,' I say. 'I've never seen two people more in love.'

Blodwen purses her lips.

'You spoilt that boy,' she says.

I smile. Blodwen has been accusing me of spoiling Owain since he was a baby.

'Too late now. No point lifting your petticoat after pissing.'

Blodwen laughs.

'And how is Nefyn?' I ask.

'Sour as ever,' she says cheerfully.

Perhaps if you'd spoilt her more she would be happier, I don't say.

'I still wish we could have joined the farms,'

says Blodwen. 'Shared grandchildren. Don't you?'

Of course I wish this. But I will never say so. Not now.

'What's done is done,' I say. 'And I love Salka.'

I have surprised myself.

But it is true.

ANWYN

Tonight we have gathered in my cousin Terfel's cottage to make rushlights. You would never know he was a good carpenter from the wretched condition of his own table and chairs.

Salka is not here. Her baby is due soon and she is tired in the evenings. Her poor ankles are swollen, and moving about is hard.

The early spring night is frosty and cold, so I have put extra wood on the fire while Terfel's grumpy wife Elen offers cider and oatcakes. Snow gathers in drifts outside the farmhouse, and Terfel goes out to shovel it away from the door. The room is smoky, and the fire spits embers onto the floor.

There is only one topic of conversation.

I don't like her

I don't trust her

I've heard she talks to the air
I've heard she dances in the dark
She sings strange songs
She speaks to plants
What do you expect? She's not from here
She runs barefoot
Her hair is damp
She talks too loud
She waves at the moon
She swims naked
She sings to the cows
I don't like her
'I do,' I murmur.

'You're soft, Anwyn,' says Sioned. 'You like everyone.'

ANWYN

When Salka sings, I feel her words in the depths of my body, though I don't understand them.

She takes me to another place, a place filled with love and lust and longing, a heartsick land of pain and sadness. When she sings, it's as if she knows all my sorrows, everything I've ever thought and felt and yearned for.

No one sings like her.

NEFYN

Will she never stop with the wailing and the caterwauling?

GARETH

We are huddled around a table in the tavern – dimly lit, as always, by the miserly innkeeper, the floor covered in damp rushes – all the boys, all friends from our youth when we were green and carefree, scaring off rooks and gathering kindling together.

Owain for once has joined us. He says the beer is on him. We refuse but he insists. 'Didn't you all buy drinks for me when times were hard? Let me return the favour. I've had a blessed year.' So we say yes.

We are laughing and telling stories. 'Remember that May Day dance?' says Huw. 'When Ifan got so drunk he passed out in a ditch?'

Terfel laughs and pokes Ifan. One of Terfel's remaining fingers is bandaged. Being a carpenter is not for the faint-hearted.

'Will we get a repeat this May?' says Terfel.

Ifan scowls. He does not like to be reminded about his drunkenness.

'Old Idris was so angry when you didn't show up at the forge,' says Huw. 'Remember how he marched through the village bellowing, "Where's that boy? I'll brand him myself."'

'And now you're the blacksmith, Ifan, and Idris is in the churchyard,' I say.

'And *you* disappeared with Sioned for an awfully long time,' says Owain, grinning.

'Didn't,' I say. 'We never left the dancing.'

'Oh yes you did,' says Ifan. 'You can't fool us.'

'That's the night I got engaged to Siriol,' says Huw. 'The next day I apprenticed to the wheelwright.'

'And Nefyn made so many flower wreaths I thought the birch branches would break,' says Terfel.

'She crowned Owain with the prettiest,' says Ifan. 'Remember?'

Owain shakes his head. 'I should go,' he says, putting down his tankard. 'The baby will be born any day now and I don't like leaving Salka alone for too long.'

There is silence after Owain leaves. We look at one another. Will anyone say out loud what we are all thinking?

I brace myself to defend my friend, who has married a strange girl who has come from away.

But no one says a word.

'Good times,' says Terfel.

Good times.

SALKA

Our son was born in front of the hearth, just before the brightening grey dawn. He slipped out so fast and easy there was no time to call the midwife. What a strange sight, a tiny male body emerging from mine into the firelight.

Owain and I both wept.

I gave him to Owain to hold, and fell asleep on the rug.

When I woke, our son was bathed and swaddled. I took him in my arms and looked into his lake eyes, blue green grey.

OWAIN

'All of our ewes have had twins! All healthy. All have lived,' I say, coming home after a long day lambing. I am muddy, filthy, tired, soaking wet, but exultant.

How is this possible? All twins, and all have survived? Ewes as well as lambs? They gave birth as easily and nonchalantly as nibbling grass.

And yet it is so.

Salka looks at me in surprise, as she holds our baby son to her breast. His fist curls around her finger.

Then she smiles at me.

'What else would they do?' she says, rocking the baby gently.

'Ewes mostly just have one,' I say.

'Ah,' she says. '*Our* sheep always have two.'

LOWRI

My mother died right after the last lamb was born. Only a witch would have known that.

SALKA

We are in the cart, going to market. The scythe blades need mending, and Owain has a fine ram to sell. I'm holding Rhiwallon in my arms, tightly swaddled, and he sleeps peacefully, lulled by the tilting wagon.

Around us the fields and hills shimmer with new corn shoots. The yellow gorse is in full flower across the moorland, and the hedgerows lining the lane are tangled with pale pink dog rose and sweet-smelling honeysuckle. Above us skylarks sing and swirl. We will stop on our return to gather armfuls of gorse for new floor and chimney brushes.

We meet Rhodri the clog-maker and his wife Nesta on the way.

They only speak to Owain. They do not look at me. Though they took the herbs I prepared for

Rhodri's swollen hand and Nesta's headaches and runny nose readily enough.

Rhodri clicks to his horse and their cart clanks away, wheels squeaking.

'Why don't they speak to me?'

Owain puts his arm around me. 'Because they are superstitious fools.'

'I did not cause Old Erin to die at lambing time. I just saw that she would,' I say.

'I know, I know,' says Owain.

Later in the market, I see faeries walking invisible through the stalls, thieving with sleight of hand. I don't know them, they don't know me, but we recognise that we are Tylwyth Teg.

One of them comes up to me and whispers, 'What are you doing with him?'

'None of your business,' I say out loud.

Owain turns to me.

'What's that?'

'Nothing,' I say. 'Just talking to myself.'

ANGHARAD

'How did Salka know?' asks Blodwen. 'How did she know when Erin would die?'

I choose my words carefully. I want no whispers of witchcraft here.

'Salka has deep knowledge,' I say. 'It's God-given how she can diagnose ailments and find the right cure. You know yourself, Blodwen, how she can bring down fevers and heal wounds. She saw sickness in Erin's face. Nothing more.'

Blodwen considers. Then nods.

'Is Salka about? I've been suffering from toothache and I hoped she might have something for the pain.'

ANWYN

I've stopped by to visit with Salka. The fields are sodden with rain and a biting wind is blowing off the mountains. No one will be working in the fields today. Owain is out checking the ewes and newborn lambs. I've already heard the marvel that all their sheep are flourishing and not a single lamb has lost their eyes to crows. Salka is making bread, and I wonder as always at her quick fingers and smooth hands as she presses and stretches the dough into shape.

Rain is pouring down and clattering against the windows. It's as if spring took fright and ran off, and winter roared back.

'I hope the cows don't take cold,' says Angharad, as she rocks baby Rhiwallon, who has lake eyes like Salka. 'We have so many new calves and the weather is harsh for spring.'

'It's raining cats and dogs today,' I say.

Salka drops the dough in the trough and runs to the door, flinging it open and letting in a blast of wind and rain.

'Hey, shut the door,' shouts Angharad.

'Where? Where?' says Salka.

'It's just a saying,' I say. 'It's not really raining cats and dogs.'

Salka looks disappointed.

'So it's not true?'

'No,' I say.

'Then why say it is raining cats and dogs when it isn't?'

I have no answer.

SALKA

Anwyn tells me she has a twin sister, Siriol, who married Huw the wheelwright last year. Before I can stop myself, I say I also have a twin sister.

The moment the words have left my mouth, I regret them.

'Do you miss her? Where is she? I bet you're the eldest,' says Anwyn.

I look at my friend, my only friend here besides Owain.

I don't know how to answer her. At these moments, I am neither here nor there. I miss my sister, and I don't miss her. She is tucked inside my memory box, where my old life is locked away.

She is gone, I say.

Anwyn nods and does not press me.

ANGHARAD

It's long past time for me to move to Downhill Cottage. My son and his wife don't need me underfoot. I've played gooseberry long enough.

A young couple need privacy, not an old woman like me shuffling around. I'm forty-three, though I don't feel such an age.

I can still come every day to lend a hand with the baby. And of course to care for the cows. (Oh, I would forgive Salka anything for the fine herd she brought with her.) Owain keeps offering to hire another milkmaid but I turn him down. The older cows like me to milk them, and I will continue until my hands are too gnarled to do so. The pride I feel in those lovely girls with their sweet faces and dark bellies, you would think I'd given birth to them myself.

ANWYN

'Why have you never married?' asks Salka. She is helping me clean out the old church floor rushes and lay fresh ones.

Salka is always blunt. I try not to be offended, because that is her way. I don't think she means harm.

What can I say? That no one has ever asked me? That I am afraid I will die in childbirth? That I like girls and not boys? That I am in love with her and no one must ever, ever know, least of all Salka?

'I am happy as I am,' I say. 'It's not easy being a wife.'

Salka looks at me. I flush red.

'What?' I say.

'Your secret is safe with me,' she says.

I don't dare ask which of my secrets she means.

SUMMER

OWAIN

The seasons pass.

One summer's day, when the lush grass sways in the breeze, the sun moves slowly across the meadows, and the air is drowsy with the hum of insects and birdcall, we go to a wedding. The wedding of our neighbour Gareth, my oldest friend, to Sioned. A wedding everyone expected. A wedding everyone has hoped for. It's been a hard winter, and everyone longs to forget their troubles for a day of merriment.

There is food and drink and joy. The bride and bridegroom beam. Everyone laughs. Everyone sings. Everyone dances to Anwyn's fiddle. Even Nefyn casts aside her scowl and sings and dances.

Everyone but my faerie bride.

Salka is silent. She sits apart at the table, her

head bent. She isn't eating or drinking. Salka, who sings all day, is silent.

I see everyone looking at her, and hear their whispers.

'She won't sing. She won't dance.'

'What's wrong with her?'

'Stuck-up cow.'

'Bad luck to bring back a witchy wife from God knows where,' says Nefyn loudly, knowing I will hear.

Salka says nothing. She sits alone, grave and quiet, hands folded. You'd think she was at a funeral, or in love with the groom.

'What are you doing? Everyone's staring,' I whisper. 'Why aren't you singing?'

Salka looks away. The shame I feel heats my blood. Why is she behaving so strangely in front of the whole village?

I can't bear it. Gareth is my best friend. Salka is spoiling his wedding.

Suddenly I am so angry I could spit. Why won't she do what I ask and join in?

'Salka! What's wrong with you? Everyone's

looking. Everyone's whispering. Don't just sit here. Get up and dance.'

SALKA

I turn to Owain, the man I love more than myself. The fateful words I must say stick in my mouth.

'I am silent because I see what's hidden.

I see what will be, not just what is.

I see sorrow for this couple. So how can I sing and how can I dance?

I am of faerie blood and I have faerie sight.

You shame me for my faerie ways. But I cannot be other than I am.

Beloved, you have struck me the first heart-blow.'

OWAIN

I don't ask what sorrow she has seen.

I would give anything to take back what I said.

How can I say I love her for her faerie ways, while upbraiding her for her faerie ways? I am no better than Nesta or Rhona or any of the village hags.

What was I thinking? How could I do this?

It must never happen again.

It *will* never happen again.

'Forgive me, Salka, forgive me,' I beg as Salka stands and leaves the tavern.

Around me the dancing and singing continues. Gareth whirls Sioned in his arms on the floor, spinning her round and round.

SALKA

I can't stay in this place a moment longer. I will choke with grief if I stay. He has not heard me. He has not understood me. I get up and hurry from the wedding feast, pushing past the twirling, stomping dancers, the drunk farmers, the merry guests.

Anwyn sees me leave and misses a note on her fiddle, then carries on playing the jig.

I need to be anywhere but here.

OWAIN

I've looked and looked and I can't find Salka. I search the house, the barns, the fields, the churchyard, then the valley, and finally climb up to the lake, where I fear she will be.

The lake gleams silver in the moonlight. I see Salka sitting on the shore by the water's edge, staring at the doorway between our worlds. The lake is wind-whipped, the shimmering water slapping against the shore. Ravens circle above hunting for prey.

Salka sits there, hugging her knees, her thin dress billowing. I sit down beside her. We huddle close together, watching the water, wild and riled and foaming.

'I'm sorry,' I say. 'I am so sorry. I would give anything to unsay what I said.'

'I know,' she says. 'Owain, I am Tylwyth Teg.

I will always be Tylwyth Teg. I will never be like people here. You must accept this.'

'I love you for your faerie ways. It will never happen again. Salka, I swear.'

She looks at me, and says nothing.

'Why have you come here?' I ask.

'The lake is my once and future home,' she says.

I feel as if she has punched me in the stomach.

'No!' I say. 'Never. Your home is here, with me, with our son.'

I start to shiver.

She smiles at me with her lake eyes.

'Myddfai is where I live,' she says. 'Where *we* live. I will stay here with you for as long as I can.'

'Don't leave me,' I say. 'Salka, don't leave me.'

She clings to me.

'Don't make me go. Oh Owain, watch your tongue, don't make me go.'

OWAIN

Five years pass. Golden, joyful years. Our kisses are sweeter than wine. Our flocks cover the hills. Our hayfields grow high as the house. Our new, much bigger house. Warm in winter, cool in summer. Our boys run wild in the fields, scaring off the jackdaws and crows, laughing, shouting, rejoicing in their beauty and their strength.

We are rich. We are blessed. We are so happy. The heart-blow I struck her is long in the past, forgiven and forgotten.

Salka is always singing. I love hearing her sing her faerie songs to our sons, their lake eyes like hers.

> *Pais Dinogad fraith, fraith*
> *o grwyn balaod ban wraith.*
> *Chwid, chwid chwidogaeth,*

Gochanwn, gochenyn wythgaeth.
Pan elai dy dad di i hela;
llath ar ei ysgwydd, llory yn ei law,
ef gelwi gŵn gogyhwg:
Giff! Gaff!
Dala, dala! Dwg, dwg!
ef lledi bysg yng nghorwg
mal ban lladd llew llywiwg.

I ask her what some of the words mean.

'It's a hunting song from long ago,' she says. 'When Daddy goes a-hunting, spear on shoulder, club in hand, he calls the swift hounds. *Giff gaff! dala dala dwg dwg.* And so on and so forth,' she says, picking up the song.

I sprawl on the floor with my back against the bed and drown in the beauty of her voice as she sings our sons to sleep.

But sometimes Salka sits by the lake, murmuring.

On moonlit nights she vanishes, and won't speak of where she's been. Other dawns she dances barefoot in the dew-soaked grass.

I know because I followed her once. She doesn't know that I know. She doesn't know that I watched.

At least I don't think she knows. With Salka, you can't always tell.

Salka is not like us.

That's why I love her, because she is not like us.

But it's hard, when Cadwgan comes home with a split lip and won't say who hurt him or why.

But I know the answer.

One of the village boys has mocked him, said he has faerie blood from his witchy mother, who has come from away.

SALKA

I slip out of bed and I run to the Lake, and I dance. I dance in the moonlight, I dance in the mist, I dance to the rustle of the water and the swishing of the reeds. I dance in the foggy dew.

I dance for my father and my sister, for my lost world.

Owain doesn't know.

Before dawn, I slip back home and slide into bed, into the warmth, into Owain.

Owain murmurs.

ANGHARAD

Salka looks so young. She has barely changed since the day Owain brought her home. To look at her, no one would believe she is the mother of three sons. Life is harsh here, and people age fast, but not her.

And not Owain. He is still the handsomest boy, the one everyone's eyes follow, my own darling son.

OWAIN

Ever since I struck Salka the first blow – the first and the last and the only, I swear by all I hold dear – I no longer bring the sheep to graze on the hills around the lake when Salka is with me. I make excuses – the grass is better on Ox Eye Moor, the Ford of the Heather is best this time of year, let's leave them grazing in the high pastures . . .

Llyn y Fan Fach should be a place of joy, the place where I first saw Salka and my life transformed, but I don't like to go too near the water, just in case . . . just in case the lake calls to her and she dives in and never returns.

SALKA

I do not regret my choice. I will never regret choosing Owain, if I live a thousand years.

I look at my beautiful Owain, running on the velvety green hills chasing our little sons, or racing through the hay meadows dodging the thistles, laughing and whooping, playing hide and seek amongst the hay bales as they are loaded onto the cart before the rain comes.

Wherever he is, I will be.

For as long as I can.

Back home, the boys take turns throwing peat on the hearth. I breathe the fire smoking warm and muddy, the scent of wet grass filling the room, and smell the bread baking, the sweet potage bubbling, and the boys playing on the floor with the toys Owain has carved for them, and I do not regret my choice.

Soft rugs now cover the flagstone floors. The wind no longer whistles under the door. Our farmhouse is much bigger and better than before. We have three bedrooms upstairs with four-poster beds instead of a hay loft. We have fine, carved linen chests and oak chairs. We have workers who help in the fields and with the animals, though Owain always tends to the sheep himself and Angharad insists on supervising the cows.

But the call of the Lake is getting stronger. It's as if I am bound to it with gossamer threads which have slowly tightened their hold, pulling me closer ever since Owain struck me the first heart-blow.

OWAIN

'Would you rather have a dirty cow yard or a clean one?' asks my eldest, Rhiwallon, as we walk through the woods gathering mushrooms and blackberries. I've strapped the baby, Gruffudd, to my back, where he squirms and gurgles.

Cadwgan, his younger brother, thinks.

'Is this a trick?' he asks.

'Just answer. Dirty or clean?' says Rhiwallon.

'Clean,' says Cadwgan. 'Less poo to shovel.'

Rhiwallon cackles. 'Wrong! A clean yard is a yard with no cattle. We are rich and that's why our yard is always dirty.'

I smile at my clever son.

I remember in the time before Salka, when our cattle yard was clean.

I shiver at the memory.

RHIWALLON

Mama says it's time.

'Time for what?' I ask, as we head across the fields up to Llyn y Fan Fach.

'Time to learn to swim,' she says, flinging out her arms and running.

'Mama, wait,' I cry out.

I'm afraid that she will vanish over the hill and I will never see her again.

Mama runs down the hill to the lakeshore. Her long black hair flies out behind her.

It's warm in the sun. I can hear our sheep calling to one another from the hillsides, and Mati barking.

Mama takes off my shoes and socks, helps me to step out of my trousers. I lift up my arms so she can pull off my smock.

'Go in,' she says.

I hold back, grab on to her skirt.

'Go on,' she says.

'I can't swim,' I say.

'You can,' she says.

She sweeps me up in her arms and walks into the water. Then she throws me in.

I scream.

As I hit the icy water, I remember. I have dreamt this. The falling and the wet dark. I sink into the lake, splashing and choking, and then . . . I am on the shiny surface, and I am swimming. It feels like the lake is holding me, bouncing me up and down.

I am light. I am air.

I'm not sure where I end and the lake begins. I don't feel cold.

'Mama, look! Watch me! I can swim!'

Mama shields her eyes with her hand.

'I see you, Rhiwallon.'

'Watch me! Watch me!'

I am a fish. I am a bird. I am a seal. I am the ruler of the waterworld.

When Mama calls to me to come out I don't

want to leave the lake.

    She dries me with her shawl.

    'Mama, how can I swim?'

    She hugs me.

    'Because you are my clever son,' she says.

GRUFFUDD

MamaDada.
   MamaDada.
   MamaDada.

CADWGAN

I had a bad dream. I come into Mama and Da's bedroom. Sometimes they let me get under the blankets with them when I'm scared.

Da wakes. Mama isn't there.

I forget my nightmare.

'Where's Mama?'

'Shh,' says Da. 'She'll be back soon.'

'Where is she?'

'Shhh. Go to sleep, Caddy.'

GRUFFUDD

Mama! Sing! Sing!

CADWGAN

Mama and I are feeding the chickens. She holds the bucket and I reach my hand inside and throw the corn as far as I can.

I like seeing the hens chasing their dinner. I don't like it when they crowd me.

'Mama, where were you last night?'

Mama smiles.

'Here.'

'No,' I say. 'Why weren't you in bed?'

Mama smiles and ruffles my hair.

'Because I wasn't,' she says. 'But I am here now and that's what matters.'

OWAIN

I know everyone gossips about her, about us. I didn't think I would care. Salka certainly doesn't. At first I didn't even notice, my head was only filled with her and we were cocooned inside our own blissful world. But as time passes, I have come up for air, and I realise I am no longer treated with the warmth that I was.

Far from it.

We aren't shunned, exactly. We are not outcasts like Wild Griff. But we are not woven into Myddfai life as we were. My mother never upbraids me, but I know she misses her friends, who have drifted into acquaintance. Gareth alone is unchanged towards me. Sioned, mostly, follows his lead. And of course there is always Anwyn, who shadows Salka like a faithful sheepdog.

My sons are greeted cautiously. They play

with each other. People fall silent when we enter rooms. No one shouts out for us to join them in the tavern. We are given a wide berth at shearings and harvest festivals.

I know that Salka gave up her world for me. But I don't think she understands that I have given up much of my world for her.

Nefyn has spread her poison well. I wish I had stopped her mouth. It's strange how love unrequited can turn so quickly to hate.

CADWGAN

Tomi says Mama is a filthy faerie. And that makes me a filthy faerie too.

I punched him.

I know Mama comes from away. That doesn't make her a faerie.

I hate Tomi and I hope he dies.

AUTUMN

OWAIN

We are gathering rushes on the moorlands for next winter's candles.

Our sons scatter across the moors and compete to see who can find the biggest and best sheaves. I bind the large sheaves together, ready to carry home. It is a full harvest moon, the best time for gathering, and the boys are thrilled to be out after dark.

'Where were you last night?' I'd vowed not to ask her, but the question has burst from me.

Salka looks away. She doesn't want to tell me. I try not to sound like I am accusing her.

Though I am accusing her.

'Please, Salka, where were you last night?'

Salka tightens her mouth. She turns to face me, and I see the fear and sadness in her eyes.

'At the lake.'

I see her sinking beneath those waters, and I want to scream.

I struggle to contain myself.

'Why?'

Salka is silent.

'Were you dancing?'

'Why do you ask?'

'Because . . .'

Because I am frightened. Because I am afraid that Salka won't come back. Because I know that my life will end without her.

But instead I say, 'What if someone sees you?'

Salka shrugs. 'What does that matter?'

'Because we live in a village and tongues wag. Please don't do it again.'

'No.'

Salka's eyes are blazing.

'Then, next time, take me with you.'

'NO.'

We work together silently, moving through the bracken. Kestrels and ravens soar above us, circling and swooping. Gathering swallows twitter in the skies. I suddenly notice that the green is

fading to brown, and the air is starting to chill.
All too soon, winter is coming.

SALKA

Why can't Owain let this be? I can't take him with me when I go to the Lake to dance. I dance in the moonlight because that is who I am, the one part of me he cannot share.

    I am a faerie. I will never be human. No matter how long I live with him upon the earth.

NEFYN

So what has hating Salka gained me?
   Nothing.
   What has my jealousy gained me?
   Nothing.
   I admit it. I will be 'Poor Nefyn' till I die.
   But if I can hurt her I will. I'm glad she will never be accepted here.
   Why should she be frolicksome and light-hearted when I am lonely and unloved?

SALKA

Owain and I are having supper with Gareth and Sioned. Sioned is not a good cook. Her roast meat is so overdone that it carves itself, and her oatcakes are always burnt. Tonight she has attempted apple dumplings.

I hope she doesn't try again.

I've learnt that humans do not like honesty. The first time I ate Sioned's food I told her it was burnt and tasted awful. She did not like hearing the truth.

Now I try to hold my tongue. I am gentle around Sioned and Gareth ever since their wedding when I saw sorrow waiting for them.

Sioned is big with child, and moves heavily. She places her hand on her lower back and I know she is in pain. The baby's foot is pressing on her ribs. I think about offering to shift the baby but I don't. She can ask for my help if she wants it.

Gareth is sitting by the fire in the armchair, and he is lost in his thoughts. Sioned asks him to put more peat on the fire, and he does not answer.

Sioned snaps at him. 'Gareth! I'm talking to you. You're away with the faeries.'

'No, he isn't,' I say. 'He is right here.'

Everyone laughs.

I don't.

OWAIN

In autumn, when the ewes were mated, the hedges laid, and the apples picked, we go to a christening. The christening of Gareth and Sioned's first child, a fine daughter they are calling Meleri, after Sioned's mother. They have tried for so long to have a child. The baby is dressed in a long white lace christening robe, which has been passed down for generations in Gareth's family. No one quite knows how they came to have such a fine robe, but now it is Meleri's turn to be swaddled in it.

Gareth holds his daughter over the font. His grin is as wide as a hearth. I have never seen Sioned look so happy. Her joy lights up her plain face.

The baby is fat and sleek as butter, and everyone rejoices.

Everyone except Salka, who sits in the pew beside me and weeps. Silently at first, and then louder.

Everyone turns around to stare.

The priest glares at her, but Salka continues to cry. Her body quivers with grief.

I am mortified.

I poke her and hiss, 'Hush, Salka, hush! Stop crying. Why are you crying?'

Salka continues to weep, as if she hasn't heard me.

I poke her harder.

'Stop it! Everyone's looking! Everyone's whispering!'

I am trembling with anger. Salka is shaming me in front of the whole village. How will I face Gareth and Sioned?

'Salka! Stop crying! Please stop crying! FOR GOD'S SAKE, SALKA, BE QUIET.'

Salka raises her tear-stained face to me and speaks so only I can hear:

'I cry because I see what's hidden.

I see what will be, not just what is.

I see the baby is not long for this world.

I am of faerie blood and I have faerie sight.

You shame me for my faerie ways. But I cannot be other than I am.

Beloved, you have struck me the second heart-blow.

One more and I return to the lake forever.'

An icy chill runs through my body. Her fateful words stab me.

I would give anything to take back what I said.

'Forgive me, Salka, forgive me,' I beg.

What was I thinking? How could I have been so quick to forsake her? I am so ashamed, so angry with myself.

It will *never* happen again.

It must never happen again.

'Forgive me, Salka, forgive me. Oh my love, forgive me.'

Salka looks at me, and the tears pour down her face.

I know that this time, she is weeping for us.

SALKA

I saw how we would end. And yet I hope – how I hope – that I am wrong.

I get up and I leave the church. I know that everyone is watching me.

I don't care.

There is only one place that I can go.

OWAIN

I am in a panic. As soon as the accursed christening is over and I have congratulated Gareth and Sioned, I run from the church to find Salka.

I go straight to the lake.

She is sitting by the shore, as I knew she would be. Mist veils the hills, and the air is damp and chill. The full-grown lambs bleat from the fields. I call out her name as I approach, breathless, but Salka doesn't raise her head, which she is cradling in her arms.

Though the afternoon is calm, the slate-grey water is turbulent, mutinous, buffeting the wild geese until they flap off, honking and wheeling across the sky. I hear the drumbeat of their wings overhead as I huddle beside Salka. The choppy water slaps against the shore as if something is stirring below, spraying me with icy drops.

I put my arm around her, and she flinches.

I am so ashamed that I start to cry.

'I betrayed you. I am so sorry. I don't know what possessed me. Oh my love, my love, forgive me, forgive me.'

Her shoulders relax.

'Owain,' she says. Her voice is silver and moss. It is still silver and moss. 'Owain, what have you done?'

'Don't leave me,' I say. 'Salka, don't leave me.'

She clings to me. As if holding me tight can stop what is happening.

'Don't make me go. Oh Owain, watch your tongue, don't make me go.'

SALKA

We are careful together. Owain watches his tongue. I see him struggling sometimes, not to reproach me, when I slip out the door on misty nights when the moon is full and do not return until dawn.

Oh, my lovely boy. If only we could go back to when our day was fair, and we could love each other freely without fear.

OWAIN

Can't we go back, to when our day was fair, and all we thought about was love?

But now I have struck her two heart-blows. Again and again, I trace back what I did, what caused me to lash out. I feel numb and fearful. The lake haunts me. I avoid Llyn y Fan Fach now, as if it were an open cesspit. I have nightmares that the lake has reared up and swallowed me, and I awake shivering and sweating.

When I look in the mirror, sometimes I don't recognise myself. There's a line across my brow, which was never there before, and my eyes have a haunted look.

And yet Salka is still here beside me, still glowing and radiant, still singing her faerie songs, still in love with me as I remain fathoms deep in love with her. I want to dissolve into her, so we will never be apart.

ANWYN

'Do you ever miss home?' I ask Salka, as we bring the cows back from the meadows for milking. I like to walk with her down the lane, following behind our sashaying cows, before the road splits and we go our separate ways.

Salka looks at me as if I am babbling nonsense. 'What?' she says. 'I am home.'

'I mean, where you came from?' I say.

'No,' she says. 'Myddfai is home. Owain is home. My sons are home.' But her face is troubled.

I ask her because she seems more detached lately, as if her thoughts are elsewhere, as if her feet are no longer so rooted to this land.

Her answer makes me glad. I don't know how I would carry on if one day I discovered that Salka had gone.

WINTER

OWAIN

The seasons pass.

Our sons slip slowly out of boyhood, growing straight and tall and strong. Even the baby, Gruffudd, is old enough to help around the farm, gathering kindling and eggs and chasing off crows from the freshly planted crops. I have carved him a little shepherd's crook of his own, which he will not be parted from. The older boys can just about manage a plough now, even if their furrows are crooked. I love hearing them call to the oxen, urging them on, praising and cajoling. They have Salka's way with animals.

If only time would hold its breath, let us freeze these moments, when our days are fair and our nights an endless delight.

ANGHARAD

I find Owain alone, chopping wood.

So I pounce.

'Is everything all right with you and Salka?' I ask Owain.

Owain looks as if I have scalded him with boiling water.

'Of course it is,' he says. 'Why wouldn't it be?'

'You seem troubled of late,' I said. 'You're my son. I worry.'

'There's nothing to worry about,' he says. 'I'm fine.'

'And Salka? Is she fine?'

'She's fine. We're all fine.'

I don't believe him.

SALKA

I watch and I wait for the third blow to fall.
Because I know, one day it will. And when it does,
I think my heart will break.

The Lake is waiting for me. I hear the waters
whispering and calling, the threads tightening.

SIONED

'It's a cold,' the doctor said. 'It's just a cold.'

Meleri sneezes. Her cheeks are flushed.

I touch her warm forehead. I look at Gareth.

'She's stopped crying,' I say. 'That's good, isn't it? Isn't it?'

'Let her sleep,' says Gareth. 'I'm sure she'll be fine.'

OWAIN

Salka opens the door and stares at the frosty lane outside our farm. 'Don't you see it?' she says quietly.

'What do you see?' I ask, peering into the freezing mist.

'A corpse candle and a funeral procession passing by,' she says. 'Heading downhill to the churchyard.'

I shake my head. I see and hear nothing but the softly falling snow. The cold stings my face.

'A death is coming,' she says.

I close the door and hold her.

OWAIN

Just before day sinks into night I hear the oxen bellowing as our sons bring them in from the field. The boys laugh and tease each other. Any moment they will stomp in, hungry and tired. They've spent the day ploughing the cold earth, getting ready for spring.

My beautiful sons.

Suddenly the passing bell rings out.

Salka stops stirring the stew. She comes over and puts her hand in mine. We listen to the chimes marking the boundary between life and death.

Dong. Dong. Dong. Dong.

The church bell tolls four times. And then pauses.

The silence crackles. Will it toll a fifth time, for a dead boy? Or stop at four before it repeats its woeful peal?

The bell stops at four.

Salka freezes. 'A girl is dead.'

Dong. Dong. Dong. Dong.

Dong. Dong. Dong. Dong.

The bell repeats, twelve rings in all.

A girl is dead.

We don't speak. We both know it's Meleri.

Sioned and Gareth's only child is dead.

The sorrow Salka foretold has arrived.

I fling on my coat, saddle a horse and ride to Gareth's, through the mist and fog. The wind howls, fighting me.

There's a single candle in the window, and I see him at the table, his head in his arms, sobbing. The front door is open, to let Meleri's soul go free.

SALKA

All that night wolves howl and owls screech and hoot. A dove flies against our window and slams dead to the ground. Thunder booms, and lightning laces the sky.

    I am afraid.

OWAIN

An icy wind blows through the fallow fields on the day of Meleri's funeral. The church bells toll through the village as we join the slow procession to the church, following behind the parish clerk as he rings the corpse-bell. Do the bells drive away evil spirits? Surely their evil is already done.

The little grave has been dug in the churchyard. The ground is so hard, it must have been quite a task.

My mother, Salka and I walk to the church through the rain, carrying sprigs of rosemary for remembrance, and take our seats.

The coffin is tiny.

Sioned's eyes are puffy and red with crying. Gareth helps her to the front, to take her seat in the place no one wishes to sit.

Everyone is weeping. Everyone is wailing.

Everyone but my faerie bride, who suddenly laughs. Salka is radiant with joy as she hums and croons.

Everyone is shocked. Everyone stares. Everyone whispers.

I am mortified.

Blood rushes to my face. My hands curl into fists. I want to shake her, scream at her, stop her mouth. 'Salka! That's enough! Everyone's looking. Everyone's whispering. Hush! Hush! A child is dead. For God's sake, how can you laugh? How dare you laugh?'

I have never felt such anger, such fury.

Salka turns to me. She is laughing no more.

'Tylwythen deg ydwi.

I am a faerie.

I see what's hidden.

Why shouldn't I laugh, why shouldn't I rejoice, when I see the baby's in a better place?

I am of faerie blood and I have faerie sight.

You shame me for my faerie ways. I cannot, I will not, be other than I am.

That, my love, was the third heart-blow.
I must now return to the Lake forever.'

OWAIN

Salka stands, and kisses my mother's cheek. My mother is astounded. Salka has never touched her before.

Then Salka walks down the aisle and leaves the church, kicking off her clogs. I run after her and grab her arm but she slips from my grasp like smoke.

Sleeting snow starts to fall.

I follow her, begging, weeping.

As she moves through the empty fields, she calls to our cows, our sheep, our horses, our sons.

SALKA

Brown cow, spotted cow, cow with no name,
Come home, come home.
Brindled cow, speckled cow,
Leave this land and come home, come home.
Wellaway. Wellaway.
Little black calf, jump down from the meat hook,
Live again.
Fat slaughtered pig, flee the butcher's knife,
Live again, live again.

OWAIN

I beg her to stay, as I watch them follow her.
    But she does not look back at me.
    Not even once.
    Again and again she calls:

SALKA

Grey oxen, stop ploughing.
Leave the field and come home, come home.
My sons, stop your toil,
Come away, come away.
Wellaway. Wellaway.
Leave this land and come home.

OWAIN

Rhiwallon! Cadwgan! Gruffudd!
  Stay! Stay! My boys! My boys.

RHIWALLON, CADWGAN, GRUFFUDD

Our mother calls, and we follow her.

OWAIN

It is as if they are deaf to me.
    I watch her go, I watch them go.
    Salka. My Salka. My faerie bride.
    Salka! Come back! Come back!
    Rhiwallon! Cadwgan! Gruffudd!
    Stay. Stay!

RHIWALLON, CADWGAN, GRUFFUDD

Our mother calls, and we follow her.

OWAIN

She never turns, she never looks back.

She leads them across the silent, frosted fields, up to the lake – my cows, my horses, my sheep, my pigs.

My sons.

I run after them, begging, pleading, hoarse from calling. Mile after mile, I follow them. Dead leaves blow across my path. The evil air spits in my face.

I follow them across the icy hillocks and frozen ditches, skidding on the moss down to the shore.

Mist lowers over the ogrish lake. White-crested waves smash onto the jagged rocks. There have never been waves on the lake before. The wind blows bitter across the churning water. Hailstones hit my head. Sleet stings my eyes.

Salka walks straight into the black water. And

with every step, she sinks deeper and deeper.

My cows, my horses, my sheep, my pigs, my sons, all follow her.

My three sons follow her and sink with her beneath the water.

My boys! Oh my boys!

Salka! Come back! Come back!

OWAIN

She was there, and then not there.
   Here, and then not here.
   The lake took back all I loved.

EPILOGUE

MATI

Where are my sheep?
   Where are my boys?
   Where is my faerie?

ANGHARAD

She's left my boy to sorrow, as I always feared she would. I try to comfort him but his grief is beyond my words. Our cattle yard is clean. Our farm grows weeds.

And yet . . . I also loved her.

But did she have to take everything? Couldn't she have left us one cow?

ANWYN

Everywhere I go, I think of her. Every note I play, I hear her voice. Every song I sing, I sing for her.
  No one will ever know.

OWAIN

Day follows day. Night follows night.

Salka has never returned.

My sons have never returned.

Salka has forsaken me.

All day, every day, I sit by the lakeshore, where my world ends and hers begins.

Around me the listless breeze drifts through the thorns. The clouds hang heavy over the barren hills.

I sit and I listen to the silence. No birds sing. I have no sheep grazing on the hillsides any more, calling each to each.

Sometimes I think I hear her voice, when the wind whispers over the water.

At twilight, I leave bread for her, the soft bread she likes.

And I tell her,

'Till tomorrow, my love. Till tomorrow.'

SALKA

Once upon a time, long, long ago,
I fell in love with a shepherd boy
with eyes as brown as silt.
He called to me, called to me, but I could not come back.
I have never forgotten him.
Rydw i'n wyllt.
Nid hawdd fy nala.
I am wild.
It's not easy to catch me.

THE END

Dacw 'Nghariad

Dacw 'nghariad i lawr yn y berllan,
Tw rym di ro rym di radl didl dal
O na bawn i yno fy hunan,
Tw rym di ro rym di radl didl dal
Dacw'r tŷ, a dacw'r 'sgubor;
Dacw ddrws y beudy'n agor.
Ffaldi radl didl dal, ffaldi radl didl dal,
Tw rym di ro rym di radl didl dal.

Dacw'r dderwen wych ganghennog,
Tw rym di ro rym di radl didl dal
Golwg arni sydd dra serchog.
Tw rym di ro rym di radl didl dal
Mi arhosaf yn ei chysgod
Nes daw 'nghariad i 'ngyfarfod.
Ffaldi radl didl dal, ffaldi radl didl dal,
Tw rym di ro rym di radl didl dal.

Dacw'r delyn, dacw'r tannau;
Tw rym di ro rym di radl didl dal
Beth wyf gwell, heb neb i'w chwarae?
Tw rym di ro rym di radl didl dal
Dacw'r feinwen hoenus fanwl;
Beth wyf well heb gael ei meddwl?
Ffaldi radl didl dal, ffaldi radl didl dal,
Tw rym di ro rym di radl didl dal.

Dacw 'Nghariad (There Is My Sweetheart)

There is my sweetheart down in the orchard
If only I were there myself
There is the house, and there is the barn
There is the door of the cowshed open

There is the magnificent branched oak
Which looks so lovely
I shall wait in its shade
Until my sweetheart comes to meet me

There is the harp, there are the strings
What am I, without anyone to play it?
There is the lively attentive darling
What am I, without winning her regard?

HOW I CAME TO WRITE SALKA

Salka started life as a cantata called *The Faerie Bride*. My friend and opera collaborator, the composer Gavin Higgins, suggested we turn the medieval Welsh legend about a lake faerie who marries a shepherd on condition he never strikes her three heart-blows into a piece for two voices, choir and symphony.

The Faerie Bride premiered at the Aldeburgh Festival in 2022 with the BBC National Orchestra of Wales, featuring baritone Roderick Williams and mezzo-soprano Marta Fontanals-Simmons – who had starred as Hel in our opera *The Monstrous Child* at the Royal Opera House – and then went on to be performed in the 2023 Three Choirs Festival.

Over a long Covent Garden lunch, I told Leah Thaxton, my wonderful editor, all about *The Faerie*

Bride, and she asked me if I'd turn the cantata into a novel. I hesitated. Not because I didn't love the story, but because I wasn't sure how to tell it as a novel. Who should narrate? Should it be Salka? Owain? Both of them? Or a third person, all-seeing narrator? I couldn't decide, so I just started writing to see what happened.

First, Salka (named after Rusalka, the Dvořák opera about a water nymph who falls in love with a prince). Her voice came to me immediately, as did Owain's, the enchanting shepherd boy she gives up her faerie world for. But love love love can be tiresome, both to read and to tell, so I knew the story needed more grit.

Fortunately, Angharad, Owain's mother, wanted to speak and had a lot to say. So I let her. I could inhabit three voices, and Angharad's thoughts about her faerie daughter-in-law would add another dimension to the tale. (In fact, she became my favourite character.)

Next, to my great surprise, Mati the sheepdog wanted a word. As a dog lover, I certainly wasn't going to say no.

After the first four voices, the dam broke, and I ended up telling Salka and Owain's story from the point of view of fifteen people.

Since I always wanted one of *Salka*'s themes to explore how insular communities project their fears and longings and prejudice onto outsiders, whose ways are other, it seemed right that the people of Myddfai should speak.

Salka enchants, enrages, alarms, disturbs. There are many versions of her story, the legend of the lady of Llyn y Fan Fach, and it's been a joy to write mine.

ACKNOWLEDGEMENTS

Salka would never have been written without the brilliant composer Gavin Higgins, who first told me about the Welsh legend of the lady of Llyn y Fan Fach, and suggested we develop it into a cantata – which we did! (*The Faerie Bride* is available on Lyrita Records.)

Next, my brilliant Faber editor, Leah Thaxton, who urged me to turn this haunting romance into a novel. Thank you, Leah, for all the help, advice, and encouragement.

Thanks also to Natasha Brown for suggesting the beautiful typeface (Adobe Caslon Pro), and to Bethany Carter, the world's most efficient and patient publicist, and the 'grown-up team', Simi Toor, Mollie Stewart, Tara McEvoy, Rosie Catcheside and Arabella Watkiss. Melissa Hyder, my gimlet-eyed and tactful copy-editor, is always a pleasure to work with.

I shrieked with delight when I saw Charlotte Day's gorgeous and atmospheric cover artwork of Welsh medicinal plants, so many thanks to her.

Thanks also to Owen Sheers, Anwyn Sheers, and Siriol Sheers, whose names I've borrowed, for many Welsh consultations, and to Dr Simon Rodway of Aberystwyth University, for casting an expert eye on the Welsh poetry, songs, and translations.

My agents at Curtis Brown, Stephanie Thwaites, Isobel Gahan and Leah Valaydon, always have my back, creatively and otherwise. Helen Mumby at the Soho Agency has been a wonderful guide for all my musical projects.

Much love always to Martin Stamp and Joshua Stamp-Simon, for sharing the adventures with me.

You can hear the Welsh folk song 'Dacw 'Nghariad (There Is My Sweetheart)', which Salka sings to her children, in a gorgeous version sung by Eve Goodman. https://www.youtube.com/watch?v=Nrkgdj0bVAo

Grateful thanks finally to my favourite banjo player and teacher, Ed Hicks, who taught me to play 'Dacw 'Nghariad' on the banjo.